Her Devoted Vampire

Siobhan Muir

ISBN: 0692701249
ISBN-13: 978-0692701249

DEDICATION

Dedicated to my husband George, who once said romance was bunk, and then graciously let me prove him wrong with this story.

ACKNOWLEDGMENTS

I have to thank the women from Embraced by Words, Morgan Kearns, Kay Phoenix, CR Moss, and Natascha Jaffa for reading through the old versions of this story. Huge thanks go to Shannan Albright for requiring me to get off my butt and publish it after she read the rough draft. Thanks to Silver James for reading the revised manuscript and fixing typos and run-ons. Thanks to Suzie Quint for catching the new errors I introduced in revisions. To Kris Norris, thank you for making this amazing cover with the picture of Fredrick I've had since the story came out the first time. Thanks most of all go to my husband, George, who always cheers me on and happily offers quirky ideas whenever I get stuck in my manuscripts. I love you.

CHAPTER ONE

Her kidnapper turned her roughly in his arms and pinned her to the wall at her back, his hands stapling hers above her head. Her nipples grew taut against the hard planes of his chest as his deep brown eyes bored into hers, his scarred face blazing with intensity.

"You're mine," he growled, and excitement shivered through her at the menace in his voice. "Never forget!"

She stared up at him and swooned.

"Oh, fuck that shit."

Bridget Shanahan damn near threw her book across the expanse of comfortable chairs and black lacquered tables beyond her own. She only refrained to keep from injuring anyone.

As if I'd ever sleep with a man who kidnapped me.

So much for suspension of disbelief. She'd picked up the cheap romance at the corner store in an attempt to cheer herself out of the funk she'd felt all week. Unfortunately, the book only served to illustrate how bleak her life was compared to the fantasy of the storyline.

What she really needed was a dark handsome knight to save her from her life.

Yeah, like I'd just trust some stranger to make life

better.

A blast of damp air gusted through the doorway of Snickerdoodles, Bridget's favorite coffee shop on the Boston Common, sending a shiver of cold down her back. The chill didn't improve her mood. She tightened her fleece scarf around her neck and grabbed her coffee cup to warm herself with a drink. Nothing but air met her lips.

Doesn't that just sum up my life right now?

She set the cup down and eyed her discarded book, but the stillness of the room made her look up. She wasn't the only one. Every woman in the coffee shop had her gaze locked on the entry, some even craning their heads to see around the potted plants and support columns. Wistful sighs erupted, providing an undercurrent to the soft conversations filled with words like "sexy", "hottie", and "handsome".

Did some sort of celebrity walk in? She scanned the person who'd walked through the door as he stepped into clear view.

Hot excitement hit her, and she trembled. *Sweet mercy.*

While not tall, the man emanated such raw power it was impossible *not* to notice him. Broad shoulders filled out the black leather trench coat that brushed his ankles, and long dark hair hung down his back from a gathered tail. A fedora straight out of the 1930s Chicago Mafia shaded his face, but she spied pale skin and a neatly trimmed dark mustache and goatee.

Her heart pounded with anticipation, and excitement made her shift in her seat as the mystery man waited patiently for his turn at the counter.

Turn around, turn around, turn around.

Bridget blinked. *What's wrong with me?* She shook off the odd spell and scrubbed her face with her hands, trying to ignore the dark stranger. The girl behind the counter served the person in front of him as quickly as possible but became solicitous and sweet as soon as the man in the hat stepped up to order. Bridget inwardly rolled her eyes even as she strained to hear his order.

I wish I could hear what he says.

Wait, what? Why in God's name did she care who this guy was or what he sounded like? He didn't look like any celebrity she knew and she'd never been into the Hollywood scene, anyway.

She snorted in disgust and jerked her attention back to her book. She fiercely told herself to read and ignore the guy in the hat and coat. *It doesn't matter that the story's unbelievable.* She managed not to hear what he'd ordered or notice where he sat down.

I'm not gonna look for him. I. Am. Not.

She could keep her eyes to herself. But someone called out "Fredrick" and her gaze tracked the mysterious man as he rose from his seat three tables away. He moved with the liquid grace of a predator and her heart fluttered with primal excitement even as her mind scoffed. The server gave him a dopey smile and held the cup out to him like an offering. He smiled back at her, took the cup then swept the whole room with his gaze as if searching for something.

Please let it be me.

Reality crashed into her skull and made her blink. *I gotta get a grip on this Miss Lonely Heart trip I'm taking.* But she didn't turn her head away.

Surprise and an odd recognition skittered through her when his gaze met hers. Eyes as dark as the night sky framed by long black lashes sucked her in until she lost track of time. She fell into those eyes, warmth and yearning wrapping around her, promising comfort to drive away the bleakness. His lips curved into an inviting smile, and he winked, sending her heartbeat into overdrive.

I want him. Bridget broke the eye contact and gave herself a mental shake. *Must pick up my book or go home before I do something stupid.*

Motion out of the corner of her eye made her turn her

3

head against her better judgment and the mystery man grabbed his jacket before approaching her table.

"Mind if I join you?"

That voice... She'd heard it before, but she couldn't place it and it did wonderful things to her insides.

"I...uh, yes, of course." She gestured to the open chair beside her.

"Thank you." He set his coffee down and settled the coat over the edge of the chair before sliding into the seat. "The book not to your liking?"

Bridget blinked. "What?"

"Your book. You keep giving it dirty looks. I take it the story is disappointing."

She grimaced and nodded. "Yeah. More unbelievable than anything else."

"Yet you've chosen a fantasy, no?"

"Even fantasy has to have an element of reality or there's no suspension of disbelief." She shrugged. "Maybe it's because I can't relate to the heroine at all. She seems...vapid."

"Vapid?" He laughed in surprise, and it warmed her from the inside out. "Excellent word. Definitely paints a distinct image."

Her mystery man's smile enticed one from her as she took in his appearance. The dark ponytail fell smoothly over one shoulder like a silk rope. She wanted to run her hands through it. It would be thick, heavy, and warm, and the scent would fill her world.

God, I'm pathetic. I should get going home now.

"I need to get going. The table's all yours."

She rose and flung her coat over her shoulders before tying the scarf around her throat. The creamy white coat was her most recent indulgence since she'd taken her job. *The book doesn't count.* The coat had enough pockets to hide receipts, ChapStick, keys, cell phone, wallet, and the pocketknife her brother James had given her. "Never go anywhere without a pocketknife," he'd told her, a problematic suggestion now that the airlines were cracking down on security since 9/11.

"I didn't mean to chase you off." He half-rose out of his chair.

"No, no. I just need to get going home. Enjoy your coffee."

And if I stay longer I might do something really stupid like give him my phone number. She shot him a dismissive smile and grabbed her own mug to drop in one of the dish bins scattered around the room. She refused to look at her tablemate with the glorious hair and forced herself to stride for the door. *I can't be this desperate.*

The cold, wet wind banished the coffee-scented heat surrounding her. She dreaded the long walk home, but she didn't have the money to waste on taxi fare. She shoved her hands in her pockets, wishing she'd remembered gloves. *Or had someone hot to hold my hand.* Bridget closed her eyes and groaned. *I've gotta get a grip.* Hell, she'd even left her book on the table. Was it worth going back for it and facing him again?

Bridget stood there on the sidewalk trying to decide what to do. The door behind her opened, but she let the sound blend into the rest of the cityscape. She sighed, shaking her head.

It's just a dime store romance I don't particularly like. Yeah, but it had been her one reward for such a shitty afternoon at work. *Oh, just bite your pride in the ass.*

Clenching her hands into fists, she whirled and slammed into her erstwhile tablemate. It was like hitting a wall, albeit a warm, delicious wall that wrapped its arms around her to steady her.

"Oh, God. I'm sorry." She rebounded, wrenching out of his grasp. "I didn't expect you to be there."

"So it seems." His voice was a rich rumble. "You left your book on the table." He held it up.

She didn't even look at it, but into his dark eyes beneath the brim of his hat. The odd recognition flared again, and she surrendered to the seductive pull of his gaze. *Why is he so familiar?* Time froze. She had no idea how long she stood there staring at him, but he never moved or questioned her scrutiny.

Chocolate brown. They're chocolate brown. She slowly came back to herself standing on a windy Boston street. *Staring like an idiot.*

"I—Yes, thank you. I was just going back for it."

She snatched the book from him more roughly than she intended, but covered her embarrassment by stuffing it into her jacket pocket. The book refused to slide in smoothly and she ended up wriggling and grunting to get it in place. *Nothing quite so sexy as a grunting woman.* At least she got to enjoy his scent. He smelled like apple spice cake and vanilla, and she desperately wanted to wrap herself up in the aromas.

Desperate being the operative word.

"I'm glad I could return it to you."

Bridget nodded. "Yes, thanks again."

Amusement curled his lips into a sexy smile. "Were you really going back for it, or were you hoping to leave it there for someone else?"

She blinked as she tried to catch up to his question. "Why wouldn't I go back for it?"

"I seem to recall you weren't overly fond of the storyline or the heroine."

"Oh, right." She grimaced with chagrin. "I wasn't, but I meant to get the book, so thanks again."

Bridget retreated from him despite her body and soul screaming to stay, to explore the possibilities of color and excitement with this familiar stranger. He proved to be observant company, and God knew she hadn't had much of that with the opposite gender. Usually men viewed her as talking boobs to enjoy or too fat to bother. It had been a long time since she'd met an attractive man who spoke to her like a person.

She almost regretted their association had to end.

"Are you walking at this late hour?" Concern laced his voice, but she didn't turn.

"Yes. Thanks." She offered no other explanation. It was none of this stranger's business why she wanted to walk home. Or had to. She forced her reluctant feet to keep going.

"Perhaps I should walk with you." He appeared right beside her, his strides matching hers. How the hell had he done that? "It's not safe to walk alone at night in a large city."

She slowed her steps and considered him, a little fear trickling into her awareness. Who was this guy, and how did he move so fast or so quietly? She stopped at the corner of an alley between two buildings. The darkness sent a warning skittering up her spine, and she stepped back into the light spilling onto the sidewalk from the nearest shop. There was friendly and then there was intrusive. She tried increasing the distance between them.

"You're absolutely right. Why should I believe I'd be safe alone with you?" She eyed him with renewed attention. "You might be one of the ones I should be protected from. Thanks, but no."

He laughed, and it wrapped around her like a warm scarf. "Certainly possible. You got it in one. I'm actually a nefarious criminal seeking illicit contact with a beautiful woman. Perhaps you'd let me hail you a cab." He gestured toward the street with one gloved hand.

When did he put on gloves? "No, thanks. I'd prefer to walk."

"I must insist, miss. If it's about money, I'd be happy to—"

She rounded on him, her fear morphing into anger. "Please don't patronize me. I don't need a man to take care

7

of me just because I have breasts. I'm fully capable of getting home on my own, thank you very much. I don't need a cab."

"Again, I must insist. My name is Fredrick MacGregor, and upon my honor as a scholar and a gentleman, I assure you, you will be safe." He tipped his fedora to her and burned her with a determined look. She half-expected him to click his heels together.

Bridget raised an eyebrow, but her gut said ignoring his warning might be like ignoring fleeing animals and the glow of a forest fire while out hiking. Unease skittered up her back as the alley seemed to breathe a fetid breath. She took another step into the light.

"Fine." She could always get out somewhere other than her apartment building to throw him off. "A gentleman and a scholar, eh? What do you study?"

"A variety of things, the most recent being comparative anatomy." Fredrick strode toward the street to flag down a cab in the infrequent traffic.

"Human anatomy?" *What was there to compare?*

"I compare human anatomy to that of other mammals." The look he threw her over his shoulder was smoldering. "Particularly the bones."

"Bones?" Bridget's unease ramped up, and she shivered.

"The bones can tell a lot about the life of their previous owner." He searched the traffic for a cab.

"Bones can't tell you about the person, their likes and dislikes." She crossed her arms over her chest. Her bones would never tell that she liked the way his shoulders fit into his jacket.

"That's true. You like to read romance, I see. Missing some spark in your life?"

Anger flared on cue. "Just because I read romance doesn't mean my life is missing anything." She wished her personal reality didn't belie her words. "Everyone likes a little fantasy. I just happen to prefer romance over Star Wars."

"No offense meant, my dear. Merely a question." He scanned the empty street.

"A loaded question. And I'm not 'your dear'." Bridget tucked her hands under her armpits in hopes of warming them. "What is this persistent belief that romance is something to be ashamed of?"

His rich laugh floated to her over the hiss of a passing car, warming her from the inside out. She hated to admit how much she liked his laughter and tried to concentrate on something else, like the scents of wet, greasy streets or damp icy wind. Somewhere a charity bell tinkled incessantly in hopes of attracting donations from the shoppers beneath the light-draped trees. The wind snuck between her neck and her scarf, and she shivered as she turned her head away from the man trying to hail a cab.

Why was he being so nice to her?

Bridget opened her mouth to ask when her eyes caught movement in the dark alley. Something about the furtive motions shot fear through her. She froze like a deer in headlights, her heartbeat increasing with each breath.

Fredrick must have noticed her stillness because he stepped into her line of sight, blocking the alley, and leaned forward to brush her ear with his mustache. The scent of spiced apples enveloped her, and calm pushed through her fear, settling her heart.

"Stay here, and wait for me."

Wait, what? One moment he'd been in front of her and the next he was gone.

The hairs on the back of her neck stood up, but she didn't know if it was from the menace in his silent movement or the dominance in his voice. Either way, excitement zinged through her as she peered into the alley and squeezed her arms tighter over her chest. Shadows moved in the alley, darker than the rest, and she swallowed hard.

Fredrick moved so fast she almost couldn't track him. He shot away from her in frightening silence and grabbed the first human-shaped shadow. It took her a moment to realize it was a man dressed mostly in dark clothing. He was larger than Fredrick, but her companion lifted him like a rag doll and flung him against a car parked on the street. He hit it hard enough to crack his head and he slid to the ground, unconscious.

Holy shit.

By then, Fredrick had already dispatched another by grabbing his collar and slamming his head into the alley wall with a heavy crunch. Bridget found her breath billowing in silver clouds as exhilaration pumped through her body. Fierce joy and an odd pride bubbled up, making her tremble. Fredrick had been completely silent and the men were huge, yet he defeated them easily.

He must have some sort of Special Forces training.

She wanted to laugh in nervous delight to express her amazement and gratitude, but someone grabbed her from behind and shoved something hard against her side as one arm snaked around her throat. The stench of wet wool and stale beer assaulted her nose.

"Fred—!" Her scream cut off as the arm tightened.

"Quiet, bitch." The voice in her ear oozed malevolence. "You're mine, and you better be quiet, or you'll be sorry."

Icy terror froze her body solid as despair cascaded through her mind. Was this how her life would end, as a statistic on the nightly news? Burning anger replaced fear as she fought to breathe through the overwhelming smell. Who the hell did this guy think he was? What had she done to him? She'd been minding her own business. Her fingers curled into claws, digging into the arm around her neck.

"You will let her go."

Fredrick's voice drifted out of the darkness in front of

them, and the arm around her throat tightened with her assailant's surprise. Bridget gasped for breath and struggled to move his arm. A new sensation made her still as something pushed deeper into her side, finally causing pain. She moaned, and her anger shifted back toward fear.

Fredrick materialized out of the darkness with the same predatory grace she'd seen in the coffee shop, and her breath stalled in prey-awareness. He stalked toward them with so much menace, she wondered if she would die right along with the jackass holding her. She knew nothing about Fredrick MacGregor. He could be a sociopath fighting this thug over his next victim.

Holy Mary Mother of God. She gasped, but couldn't breathe. Blood roared in her ears, and little fireflies of light appeared at the edges of her vision.

"Let her go, and I may let you live." Fredrick's voice escalated her fear, old as death and cold as a grave in the wet earth.

"Fuck off, asshole. Get your own bitch to screw."

"She is mine, so I suggest you let her go, and find someone else to trouble with your juvenile tendencies."

Bridget wanted to protest anyone's ownership of her person, but pain and suffocation overwhelmed everything else.

"Tell you what." Her assailant jerked her backwards and tightened his grip on her throat. "I'll take her first, and you can have her when I'm done."

Fredrick laughed, but the sound was eerie and hollow. "I'll say it again, but this is the last time, so listen closely. Let her go, and I may let you continue to breathe. Harm her, and my decision will be made. The choice is yours."

Fredrick couldn't move fast enough to counteract the knife in Bridget's side, but she didn't have the breath to tell him. The arm around her throat tightened once more, and the blackness at the edges of her vision snuffed out the fireflies. She had to stay upright. If she fainted while in this guy's grip, she'd never escape. She tried to struggle, but her body felt like lead weights had been tied to her limbs.

"Suck my dick, shithead!"

Fredrick let out a hiss, and his eyes glowed red for a moment. Or maybe she was just hallucinating from lack of oxygen.

Fredrick lunged at her so fast he simply disappeared from where he'd been standing. The man behind her tried to yank her around while he thrust the knife into her side. Searing pain screamed across her awareness before she hit the ground when the thug shoved her away from him. Fredrick ended up somewhere behind her and the thug screamed, but cold seeped into her from the icy cement. The blackness swallowed her sight as her breath ran out, and the sound of roaring blood filled her descent into silence.

CHAPTER TWO

"Suck my dick, shithead!"

Black fury welled up inside Fredrick with the thought of this unwashed, ignorant churl holding the woman who smelled of pine forests in the sun. He hadn't learned her name, but she'd been the bright spot in the early evening hours since he rose. He woke with her face in his thoughts and a feeling of imminent danger surrounding her. Now, danger had her by the throat, and his rage spread through his limbs, fueling his hunger.

He leaped at the man and the woman stiffened for a moment as the bastard shoved a weapon into her side, then yanked it backwards through her flesh. *You will pay for that.* Fredrick grabbed the woman's arm and jerked her away, the knife coming free. He snarled as he reached for the man's throat. She dropped bonelessly to the concrete as Fredrick hauled the screaming man toward him and sank his fangs into his neck.

The thug gasped, and his body went rigid as Fredrick sucked all his hot, sweet blood out of the carotid artery.

"No, no, stop…" The man's resistance waned as Fredrick dragged him down the alley, weakly protesting.

"You chose." Fredrick snapped his neck, dropping the

corpse into a handy dumpster.

He carefully wiped his mouth with his gloved hand and tore out of the alley to gather the woman into his arms, hoping no one had noticed her lying on the sidewalk. He listened as the blood revitalized his body. Even with the nourishment, he didn't think he could turn so many minds away from the incident.

Fortunately, no one had come out of the coffee shop in the few moments of the attack. He was grateful the humans of Boston were too busy to see his woman bleeding to death.

There's something wrong with me if I'm grateful no one noticed.

A wide dark stain spread over the left side of her jacket and panic pounded in his skull. The scent of warm rusty blood perfumed the air and he almost swooned. *Damn, she even smells good when dying.* He rolled her gently, snarling under his breath as he scrutinized the damage. Her whole side had been torn from her hip almost to her spine, the ragged flesh shifting with each breath. *Goddess, protect her.*

Fredrick lifted her in his arms and strode along the Boston street, projecting invisibility. He wasn't really invisible, he merely projected a suggestion to passersby there was nothing of interest to see, and their gazes slid away. Three women chattering excitedly about a recent shopping experience sauntered past him without a second glance at him and his human burden.

Fredrick reached his black Aston Marten Vanquish S and clicked open the doors. He laid his woman gently in the passenger seat and unwound her scarf from her neck. *Must slow the bleeding.* He packed the scarf against the wound track and held her coat over it, tightening the seatbelt around her. He shook his head at the destruction of the leather from her blood. *I'm sure Szilivia will know someone who could get it out.* He leapt over the car and slid behind the wheel, starting the ignition with a deft flick of the wrist. *Oh, Goddess, please let her hold on until we get home.* A little voice suggested he should probably take her to an emergency room, but his possessive instincts rose in fury. No one would touch her without his knowledge. One human too many had already touched her. He'd be damned if he let some ignorant hack take her away from him.

He slammed the accelerator to the floor and tore into traffic. Panic lit his gut as he sensed her body sliding toward death with each second, her heat dissipating in the air of the passenger cabin. If they could make it to his home in Gloucester in less than twenty-five minutes, he'd have a chance at saving her. He tapped his cell and dialed, gritting his teeth as he waited for Szilvia to pick up.

"Come on, come on, pick up the damn phone." He jerked the wheel, and the car skidded onto Massasoit Road off Highway 133.

"MacGregor Residence," Szilvia's voice answered pleasantly.

"Szilvia, prepare clean water, biodegradable thread, sterilized needles, and lots of clean cloths ready in the infirmary."

"Fredrick? What did you do?" Surprise shifted into disgust.

He'd been known to make a few mistakes in the past, but this was hardly the time to rehash them.

"I'll tell you when I get there. I'm already at Samoset and coming in. Be ready."

He ended the call and concentrated on the dark road winding through the winter forest. His driveway sat near the end of the development beside the river, an elegant wrought iron gate stretched across it. The gate swung open just in time for him to slip through. He checked on the unconscious woman beside him. She was still alive. He sensed her heartbeat like the bass thump of a warped techno song, but it had slowed.

"Hold on. Just hold on a little longer," he whispered.

His old brownstone stood on the Little River, not quite the last house on the road, but it had sufficient grounds to let him live in peace. *And let the werewolves run.* He skidded to a stop in the horseshoe-shaped drive and shot out the door, a determined calm settling over him. He'd made it home in less than twenty-five minutes, but she'd faded faster than he'd hoped. He damn near ripped the passenger door off its hinges and knelt beside the woman lying in the seat.

Please be alive, please be alive. An odd chant for a vampire, to be sure, but something he wished for more than anything.

She moaned softly when he touched her, and his gut clenched.

"Easy, almost there." He cradled her against his chest as he pulled her from the car. "I've got you. I'll take care of you."

The scents of fresh blood and autumn forest assaulted his nose, but there was less blood on his seat then he expected. The information barely scratched the surface of his awareness as he strode to the side door of the mansion. He slammed through, chastising himself for enjoying the scent of the victim in his arms as he carried her into the infirmary.

But, damn, she smells so sweet.

Szilvia, Cynthia, and Matt awaited him with the supplies he'd requested. Szilvia's disgusted expression hardened at the sight of his burden, but the others tilted their heads in curiosity.

Fredrick laid the woman out on the table and gently peeled apart her coat. The brush of his hands against her skin sent shivers racing over him. *Why is she so electric?* He tugged her arms from the sleeves, wishing he could do more, but Matt's inhale through his nose reminded Fredrick of the others in the room.

"Where did you find her? She smells wonderful." Matt pulled the jacket away from her body and raised it to his nose. "Sweet."

"Boston." Fredrick shoved the spike of possessiveness away.

Matt raised his eyebrows, and the women gaped, startled.

"You went to Boston tonight?" Szilvia asked.

"Whatever for?"

Fredrick gritted his teeth against his PA's disdain and shifted around the table to remove the delicious woman's boots. *Why is this such a big deal?*

"You had to go to Boston to get a good meal and sex. You couldn't simply find it here in Gloucester?"

"They say some of the best seafood is in Boston." Cynthia's lips curled with amusement as she prepared the antiseptic and needles. "But she doesn't smell like sex."

"I didn't have sex with her, we had coffee." Fredrick dropped the first boot on the floor and moved to the next one.

"Coffee." Szilvia's voice had the humidity of the Gobi desert. "You went all the way to Boston to have coffee with some random woman?"

"No, I went all the way to Boston to check on Snickerdoodles and ended up having coffee with this woman."

Szilvia leveled him with an icy stare. "I'm not helping you with a She-Meal."

Fredrick's lips pulled back from his canines, but Matt's appreciative whistle stilled the snarl in the back of his throat. Matt had pulled the scarf away and opened the woman's shirt. He'd revealed her breasts pressed hard enough against the lycra fabric of her bra to show her nipples. Despite the confining undergarment, her breasts were full and rounded like ripe cantaloupes. Fredrick imagined pressing his face against their fragrant swells, and

17

his body responded to his thoughts. *Think of something else.* His mind helpfully served up an image of her glorious breasts in the softest Hungarian lace. Blood red to complement her strawberries-and-cream skin. *Not helping.* He estimated the enticing mounds to be cup size D, perfect for nuzzling and suckling. Combined with the sounds of her pleasure, he'd be her slave forever. But Matt's murmur of appreciation of her glorious body dragged his mind back to the present. *Mine.*

"Roll her onto her right side." He forced his thoughts toward moving furniture or mowing the extensive lawns outside his home. Anything to keep from ripping Matt's throat out and his cock from announcing itself. "She's been cut beneath the ribs. It's deep. We have to get the blood stopped before she dies."

"What's so important about this She-Meal?" Szilvia flipped her white-blonde braid behind her shoulder and planted one hand on her hip. "There are plenty of them in Gloucester. She doesn't look too different from the rest of the Ameri-trash around here."

Szilvia's disdain grated on his ears, but he held his temper in check with iron willpower. *You can't slash her throat. You need her.* Maybe, but she was fast becoming less important by the moment.

"I thought you said she had a stab wound."

Cynthia's statement brought Fredrick around to her side. The woman on the table had sustained an injury, but only a rough pink scar remained. *What the—?* It looked as if it had occurred days ago rather than hours. Fredrick scanned her body, listening to her heartbeat. It had stabilized and settled into a steady, strong rhythm.

His gaze shot to her face. Who was this woman? She healed like one of the Elder Races. His vision hadn't warned him about her abilities or her possible species, only that he needed to defend her from danger.

"Who is she?" Cynthia echoed his internal question, her brown-gold eyes glowing in the light. "She's not a werewolf, and she doesn't smell like a vampire or a Hell Hound."

He shook his head. As the Luna, the Alpha female of the Gloucester pack, Cynthia would know the majority of the Elder Races in the area. As head of Fredrick's security team, she made it her business to know. He trusted her nose over anyone else's.

Maybe she's an earth elemental.

"She's not a vampire." Fredrick shook his head. "I'll have to do some research, but at the moment, we'll have to consider her something akin to the Elder Races. This definitely explains the vision I received to go after her."

"You had a vision about her?" Szilvia's eyebrows rose as she shot a look at the woman on the table.

"Yes." He brushed the woman's hair away from her cheek and Szilvia scowled.

Szilvia held the position of Fredrick's personal assistant and chamberlain. She oversaw all of his many financial interests, and her expertise in management showed profitable results. However, her attachment to him grew in proportion to her disdain for his "She-Meals", as she called them. If he didn't know better, he'd suspect she was jealous of his search for blood and sex beyond her. She'd once admitted her love for him, but his own feelings never mirrored hers, and he'd never wanted to bind her to him by feeding from her.

Szilvia doesn't deserve that.

"So she's why you went tearing out of here earlier." Matt nodded slowly. "I can see why. If she's not a werewolf or vampire, and she's definitely not human, what is she?"

"Maybe she's Fae." Szilvia tilted her head to scrutinize the woman.

"No, she doesn't smell Fae." Cynthia sponged the dried blood off the woman's side. "In fact, she doesn't smell like anything I've encountered before." She inhaled again. "But she definitely smells good."

"Let's get her cleaned up and into a bed." *Too bad it isn't into mine.* Fredrick busied himself with drying the woman's skin where Cynthia had washed. "Cynthia, will you help her get undressed when we're done? I'll do some research and maybe we'll figure out what she is. If not, we can ask her when she wakes up."

He slowly dragged the soft towel over her side, pretending not to notice when his fingers extended beyond the fabric. One brush of her skin reenergized his erection, and he had to take his hand away before the others noticed. Cynthia raised an eyebrow, but said nothing as she examined the wound track. The woman's regenerative qualities turned the scar into nothing but a thin pink line running from just above her left hip almost to her spine.

"Wow." Cynthia met Fredrick's amazed gaze. "Think she'll wake soon?"

Fredrick shrugged and shook his head. She seemed to be breathing easily and her heartbeat remained strong, but she showed no signs of coming around.

"So what's her name?" Matt asked as he separated her clothing into ruined and salvageable.

"I don't know."

"You don't know?" Szilvia's acidic voice cracked. "You said you shared coffee with her. Why would you rescue a bleeding She-Meal and bring her here when you don't know her name?"

"I didn't have time to ask."

"Oh for the love of Istvan." Szilvia threw her hands up and strode out of the room.

Szilvia's disgust didn't faze Fredrick. He had plenty of time to learn the name of his vision. She lay before him and he'd never let her go now that he'd found her. He'd seduce it out of her with love, caring and—

"Check her wallet. I'm sure she has some sort of identification on her. They generally do these days." Cynthia handed Fredrick the ruined coat with a smirk.

Oh, right. He hid his chagrin by rummaging through its pockets.

He pulled out the book, soaked in her blood, and tossed it aside. It hit the floor with a wet thud. More searching revealed a cell phone with a cracked screen, ChapStick, a set of keys, a pocketknife, and a simple nylon wallet. He snatched the wallet and opened it to the ID carrier, his hands shaking in anticipation.

The name printed in bold black letters at the top of the card read, "Bridget Shanahan." Satisfaction rolled through him. *Hello, Bridget.*

CHAPTER THREE

Bridget opened her eyes and sat up with a gasp. Fear and adrenaline coursed through her and her heart thundered in her chest as she tried to catch her breath.

I'm okay. I'm okay. The repeated mantra settled some of her nerves as she searched the world around her for danger. The room around her appeared quiet and empty. Plush chairs and lacquered tables filled the space, but no one sat at any of them. She shifted her feet to the floor, momentarily tangling them in her glittering emerald skirt.

Hello. Why am I wearing a dress?

Surprise faded to curiosity as she fingered the smooth silk fabric covering her body. When did she get this dress? And why did she look like she'd woken up at a swanky dinner party? She untangled her shoes from the skirt. She extended one leg and admired a shimmering Lucite heel strapped to her foot. Even her toes sported emerald green nail polish.

Who am I dressed as, Cinderella? Maybe the ball would start any minute. *Heh, now all I need is a pumpkin and a prince.*

Soft music played from the speakers recessed around the room, and warm golden light poured from the track-lighting above the counter. The display case shelves held row upon row of decadent pastries, and the scents of cinnamon, chocolate, and coffee met her nose.

Am I back in Snickerdoodles?

Bridget scanned the room for something familiar, but everything seemed off kilter, as if the lines of the room didn't quite match up. It was enough to keep her seated. *How sexy would it be if I toppled off my heels?* She leaned forward to see the windows around a large potted palm, and a soft, cream-colored, cashmere shawl fell off her shoulder, covering her hand.

What the—

Her eyes caught on a spreading crimson stain marring the creamy color. She lurched to her feet and threw the shawl away from her, praying she hadn't ruined her dress or the leather sofa. Where had the blood come from? Panic flooded through her as tears sprang to her eyes. Intense pain stabbed her side and she gasped, her knees buckling. She collapsed back onto the couch and groaned, clutching her ribs with one hand.

What had happened? One moment she'd been reading a kitschy romance novel in the coffee shop, the next she reclined on a leather couch. In the same coffee shop. Dressed for an evening on the town with a bloody shawl and a body injury.

Yeah, that makes sense. 'Cause I'm always going to swanky parties in coffee shops. She shook her head, but the pain remained. *Wait, I forgot the book, didn't I?*

"Bridget! Bridget Shanahan!"

Her head jerked up at a man's voice shouting her name. Her pain receded as a blast of cold air buffed her bare shoulders and she shivered. A man dressed in an elegant tuxedo with an emerald green cummerbund and bowtie bolted into the room. He scanned the space and damn near knocked over several chairs when he spotted her. He threw himself to his knees in front of her, his black trench coat fanning around his legs like a cape.

"Holy Goddess, are you all right, my dear?"

She stared at him blankly. He looked familiar, but she couldn't place him.

"Bridget. Tell me you're all right." He settled his hands on her arms.

"Uh—"

He slammed her into his embrace, squashing the stuffing out of her. "I was so worried. You've been on my mind for weeks." He pushed her back to look her over. "Are sure you're all right?"

"I—"

"Good Goddess, what happened to your shawl?" He released her and picked up the bloody garment. "There's blood here." He swung his gaze back to her, scanning her body for injury. "Are you hurt? Is this your blood?"

His words rumbled with a subtle Scottish burr that made her heart flutter and warmed her from the inside out. A mixture of apple spice cake and vanilla filled her nose and sparked a memory of a blustery Boston street. Wait, when had she been outside?

"I don't know."

The intensity of her pain had faded, but tension in her ribs warned her not to make any sudden moves.

He dropped the shawl and gathered her back into his arms, squeezing gently. Bridget sighed and closed her eyes, quite content to be pressed against his warm, delicious chest. *I'll just rest here for a moment.*

"So, you're not hurt?" He pushed her back too soon and stared at her intently with his chocolate brown eyes.

Those eyes.

"Bridget?"

"Oh, uh, sorry. I'm a little shaken up, but I'm okay. Really."

"I'm so sorry I was late. I had some last minute issues come up with one of the shops." He stood and offered her a hand up. "I had to renegotiate the deal on the coffee from that California farm, and they insisted they hadn't used pesticides." He snorted. "My investigation said different. It was a mess."

"Oh, good." *Coffee?* "I'm glad you made it." *What?* "I just need to get my bearings."

She swung her gaze to the ornate grandfather clock at the end of the counter and felt bone-deep sorrow at the time on its face. Tonight had been her debut, and now they were at least an hour late. It might not be New York, but the Boston Elder Society didn't wait for anyone.

Hang on, debut? Boston Elder Society?

She shook her head and rubbed her cheeks with her hands. None of this made any sense. She'd never been part of any high society in Boston, and she swore she didn't know this man as well as he seemed to know her.

"You're not fine." He wrapped an arm around her waist. "Here now, let's get you into a chair, and I'll get you a cup of something warm. Tea or coffee?"

"I have no idea what's going on."

She tried to pull away, still shaking her head. Dizziness assailed her, and her legs gave out again, making her slump against him.

"Easy now, almost there. I've got you. I'll take care of you."

He scooped her up in his arms, cradling her against his warm chest and carried her over to a fluffy armchair with burgundy upholstery. Light glinted off something on his chest, and she fingered a silver lapel pin over his heart. It had the shape of a tree with spreading branches and roots in a circle of silver. The design seemed familiar to her as if she'd seen it somewhere before, but the memory refused to focus.

One thing was very clear. She liked to be in Fredrick's arms. She liked it a lot.

Fredrick, that's his name. The memory of a blustery

street and a discussion about anatomy came into focus.

"You're Fredrick, right? Fredrick MacGregor."

He chuckled. "Who else would I be?"

"Uh…"

Despite her uncertainty, she didn't want him to release her. But he set her down in the soft chair and strode swiftly to the counter as if he owned the place. She watched his ponytail slide across his shoulders as he prepared her hot drink, not sure if he'd chosen coffee or tea. His hair reminded her of the Stanton-bred quarter horse stud someone had bequeathed to him for his charitable help on their behalf.

Stanton-bred quarter horse?

Bridget groaned. Where were all these memories coming from? She'd never been wealthy or part of some sort of high society. Confusion swamped her. She lived in Boston and worked as a project manager, didn't she?

Her questions popped like soap bubbles when Fredrick returned and draped his trench coat over her. The coat held heat and the scents of the man who'd worn it, a strangely comforting combination.

"You looked cold, love." He brushed her cheek with the back of one finger. "I'll have your coffee in a minute, and we'll make the best of this mess."

"Okay."

He gave her an approving half-smile that melted her heart, and he retreated to the counter where the coffee maker percolated in happy industriousness.

Bridget pulled the coat around her shoulders and wriggled down into the chair. Her pain seemed to be gone and she was able to focus a little better. But it had been a long and trying day, and she didn't want to go to a fancy coming-out party, anyway.

Fredrick can always introduce me to the Elder Society later. Wait, introduce her for what? She was no one special. She rubbed her eyes with the heels of her hands in the vain hope she could scrub reality back into place. When her gaze refocused, she still sat with his spice-cake-scented coat over her and the sounds of the coffee brewing. The soft music played a counterpoint, and a periodic rumble of a furnace accompanied the breeze of warm air brushing the tendrils of hair at her neck.

Something wasn't right. She frowned as she tried to focus her memories. She'd left Snickerdoodles to go home and forgotten her book on the table with Fredrick. When did she make plans to go out with him? *I don't remember meeting him before, but it feels like I've known him forever.*

"Fredrick, how long have we been together now?"

He glanced at her over his shoulder as he poured coffee into two mugs. "What an odd question, love. We've been together for six months."

Bridget shook her head. No, no, that couldn't be right. *I just met him last night, didn't I?*

"I can't seem to remember the first time we met." She closed her eyes and leaned her head back against the chair. "Are you sure it's been six months?"

Fredrick's hand settled on her knee, and she cracked her eyes open. He held a cup of coffee out to her, and she worked one hand free of the trench coat to grasp it. Heat seared her palm, and she hissed, adding the other hand on the handle.

"Thank you."

"You're welcome, love." He watched her drink with his head cocked to one side, a small smile hovering over his lips. "Of course I'm sure. I'd never forget the day we met."

She sipped her coffee. "Mmm. Tell me what you liked about it." Maybe it would help her remember it too.

"It was a dark and stormy night…" He waggled his eyebrows.

She almost snorted her coffee. "Yeah, yeah. This is Boston. Most autumn nights are dark and stormy."

"Very true. But this one was particularly stormy, like

27

your eyes when I frustrate you." He grinned to show he teased.

"Yeah, you're good at that." She frowned at her coffee cup. "But for our date...we never got to dance, did we? I really did want to dance with you."

Wait, what? Dancing in a coffee shop?

"Well, now, that's easily remedied. We can dance right here if you're feeling up to it."

"Here?" Bridget looked around the room and found an open space where chairs and tables had stood just moments before. *Where did they go?*

"Right here. Right now." Fredrick took her cup and set it down, then peeled his jacket away from her. He offered her his hand as he raked his gaze over her body, his smile widening with approval.

Gathering her courage and her strength, Bridget grasped his hand and slowly rose to her feet. Her side gave a minor protest, but once she stood, the pain dissipated. The silver lapel pin winked at her as he turned and led her to the open parquet floor. Despite her caution, she still managed to trip on her Lucite heels.

Fredrick pulled her into his arms, holding her steady until she could get her feet. Bridget had the odd sensation he protected her from more than just the floor.

"Easy now, I'm here, Bridget. I'll always be here from now on." He hugged her like he held spun glass, laying a soft kiss on her forehead. "I'll never leave you unprotected again. I promise you."

Bridget released a sigh and snuggled into his embrace, reveling in the warmth and solidity of his body. She closed her eyes and inhaled his scent. Was this a dream? It felt and smelled real, but what about all her unclear memories? *Who cares as long as he holds me like this?*

He pressed his lips against her temple. "I promise to care for you forever."

Forever seemed too short a time, and she pulled her

head back to tell him.

Dizziness hit her again, and she sagged against Fredrick's chest with a groan. Her ears rang with white noise, and she fell into it as her stomach lurched. She closed her eyes, willing her stomach to settle as something jostled her body for a few moments then stopped. Fredrick's comforting presence had disappeared, and she sat all alone.

So much for protecting her.

But was she really in danger? Memory moved like thick mud, but unease sang through the murk, warning her of big, impending changes. What had they been?

The warning became clearer. She concentrated on it, and her awareness sifted through the viscous sludge, drawing closer to the source. Individual sounds separated out until she could distinguish the spaces between the words, but not the words themselves. The voice sounded familiar and male, but the tones were hysterical, as if the owner grappled with fear.

She immediately wanted to sooth the insistent fearful qualities and worked hard to pull herself closer through the thick fog. Sounds intensified, and light pierced the murk in ragged slashes, demanding her attention. Bridget struggled to reach for the light, but her body felt weighed down. It took so much energy to fight and she almost let herself sink away from it.

I'm so tired. She could just let go and rest. No one needed her. *Wait, what? No. Help!*

She didn't want to fall into the darkness again. She didn't want to be trapped there forever, lost in the black blankness. She screamed her silent terror, and the voice she'd heard reached deep down into her darkness and wrapped a cord of bright light around her, dragging her back to consciousness.

"Bridget Shanahan, come back to me."

I'm coming. Don't let me go.

"Hold on. I'll help you if you just reach for me."

She struggled against the dark, stretching her hand as far as it would go...

"Uhnnn." Bridget groaned and slowly opened her eyes.

Light speared her sight, and she squinted until the pain receded. Details of the room around her settled into solidity. Her gaze took in an elegantly decorated room in warm colors. A burgundy bedspread weighed down her body over emerald green satin sheets. One brick wall stood beyond the oak footboard and made a solid background to the man seated in a chair at her bedside.

Bridget immediately recognized her erstwhile dance partner from Snickerdoodles, and her heart fluttered with excitement. She'd shared coffee with him, and now he sat here in her bedroom. She frowned. Why was he in her bedroom? Her gaze snapped to the bedspread again.

This isn't my bedroom.

CHAPTER FOUR

"Where am I?" Bridget struggled to sit up, but aborted the effort when pain shot through her side. "Oh, shit."

"Just rest for now. You aren't ready yet." His familiar voice settled some of her uncertainty and fright.

She took a deep breath. "Why do I hurt? What's wrong with me?"

The ache in her side felt like she'd been clobbered by a mobster thug wielding a baseball bat. *You want I should break her kneecaps, boss?* The pain hadn't been this bad when she'd woken up on the couch in the coffee shop dream. *It was a dream.* Disappointment speared through her, but she shoved it away to test her injury beneath the sheets. She couldn't feel anything beyond bruised.

"Do you remember me, Bridget? I met you at Snickerdoodles." Fredrick laid a hand on the bed.

Oh, she remembered, all right. She remembered the scent of his skin and the warmth of his body beside her. At least, she thought she did. He'd wrapped his trench coat around her, hadn't he? *That was the dream.*

She closed her eyes and shook her head to clear the cobwebs of mixed memories.

"I returned your book and tried to hail a cab for you.

Do you remember that?"

No, that's not right. We danced. Wait. Yes, she remembered the terrible kidnapping scene in the book and how she'd left it on the table in the coffee shop. Her memories played out in a reel until it ended with red eyes and searing pain.

Bridget's eyes flew open, and she stared at her companion with dawning unease. That hadn't been in the dream. His expression filled with concern and compassion, his eyes a deep chocolate brown. No sign of red anywhere. They weren't even bloodshot.

"You're Fredrick MacGregor, the scholar who likes anatomy."

"That's right." A smile flitted over his lips.

"And you smell like spiced apples and vanilla."

His black eyebrows disappeared into his hairline, one tendril falling across an eye. It looked soft and smooth, and she wanted to push it behind his ear for him.

"Spiced apples and vanilla, hmm?" His smug look banished any tender feelings that might have developed.

She grimaced. "Where am I and what am I doing here?"

"You were stabbed in the side, and I brought you to my home here in Gloucester to take care of you."

Stabbed? That would explain the bruised feeling in her side. She wrenched the emerald bedclothes away from her body and scanned the skin of her torso. The bruised pain she felt directed her eyes to her left side, but nothing marred her skin, not even discoloration. *Or clothes, for that matter.* What was she doing in a stranger's house, naked? Then the rest of his words sank in.

"Wait, did you say Gloucester?"

"Yes. It was the safest place I could think to take you."

Bridget narrowed her eyes as she raised her gaze to meet his.

Safe for whom, you chocolate-eyed kidnapper?

"Normally you take injured people to the hospital. Or at least call the paramedics." She dropped the covers. "Not bring them to…to…"

"A comfortable and richly decorated bedroom?" He raised an eyebrow.

"Yes." Was it his bedroom?

There are worse places to be, a traitorous voice remarked.

"Would you rather I took you to a cold, impersonal, and sterile room with white walls and hollow-eyed doctors?" Before she could respond, he waved such a thought away. "There was no time, and I knew I could care for you better than any human hospital."

Riiiiggghhhtt, that's what all the sociopaths say to their victims.

"I have to get home." She'd make it home come hell or high water. She sat up and slid her feet from the covers. Goosebumps zinged along her leg when it hit the open air.

"Whoa!" She jerked her legs back under the emerald sheets and stared incredulously at the man sitting next to her bed. "Where are my clothes?" *And that sexy dress?*

"I haven't had time to get any from your apartment." His eyes never dropped from hers. "I'll send someone presently."

She raised her eyebrows. *Odd turn of phrase.* "How do you know where I live?"

"Your driver's license had all your information."

She groaned, frowning. "Of course it did. Can't someone lend me some clothes so I can get home? No need to make a special trip."

"I'm afraid that's not possible at this time." He gave her an apologetic smile.

"Why not?" She narrowed her eyes.

"You need to rest and it's not safe."

"Not safe? How is it not safe for me to go home?" She paused. "Please don't tell me I'm actually the daughter of some CIA sleeper agents, and the government just has to have my help deciphering a secret message like the plot of some B-rated action flick."

Fredrick laughed. "No, nothing so fanciful, but that's quite inventive." He shook his head and sobered. "No, it's far more nebulous than that."

"That's just great. A perfect ending to a perfect day." She sighed, slumping back in the bed. "Stabbed, kidnapped, and naked in a stranger's bed. It just doesn't get much worse."

"Except, perhaps, being kidnapped by a vampire with a house full of werewolves." He shrugged, a half-smile curling his kissable lips.

She snorted. "Thank God there's no such thing as vampires or werewolves."

He stilled as if the life within him bled away, leaving nothing but a quiet, waxen shell. His face lost the humor in it. Unease crept through her as she stared hard at him, clutching the covers so tightly her knuckles turned white. The scent of spiced apples shifted to a dirt smell, like moist earth or the desert after the rain. A shiver worked its way up her spine and her stomach cramped.

Again with the teasing. Ugh.

She cleared her throat. "Right, well, thank you for whatever you did. I kinda remember being stabbed. It hurt like hell. How bad was the damage, and how long have I been here?"

Life seeped back into him as he cocked his head to one side, his eyes narrowed in consideration. "You have only been here a few hours, but we didn't do anything other than look at your wound. You healed all by yourself."

"Yeah, I know I'm healing. I just want to know what you did to close the wound and how many stitches I needed."

"I told you. We didn't do anything. Your body healed on its own."

She lifted the bed sheets away from her body again to get a better look at her left side. The skin appeared a little pink at her waist, but nothing suggesting a stab wound. She looked back up at him, anger coiling. "How long did you say I've been here?"

"Only a few hours."

"That's impossible. No one can heal that fast. What kind of game are you playing?"

Fredrick shook his head. "No games, Ms. Shanahan. Your body had already closed the wound when we got you here." His gaze sharpened. "I would like to know why you managed to heal so quickly and what gave you this ability." He frowned. "But it appears you didn't know you could do that."

"Of course I didn't know I could do that." Bridget released the bed sheet to her waist. "No one can do that outside of science fiction novels."

His gaze dropped to her chest, and a predatory expression flooded his features. An odd combination of exhilaration and lust zinged through her, which only pissed her off more. She growled and jerked the sheets back up.

"Nice."

He coughed and had the grace to look chagrined. "Forgive me, but I've found it very difficult to turn down an opportunity to view such beauty."

"Focus, Mr. MacGregor. You brought me here, and I wake up to find myself naked with a stranger asking me how I can heal like…like—"

"Like the Elder Races."

Bridget blinked. "The what?" *Why does that sound familiar?*

"Elder Races, vampires and werewolves."

Okay, this guy has completely lost his mind.

She blinked at him. His lips tightened, and he shook his head with a sigh before he rose and strode across the room to a small bureau. She watched his ass the whole way, trying not to appreciate how well his jeans fit. His legs weren't bad, either.

Now who needs to focus?

She missed what he'd picked up, but caught sight of her pocketknife when he flipped open the longest blade and held it against his palm. Before she could say anything, he dragged the blade across the flesh of his hand.

"What are you—?"

He hissed in pain, but very little blood flowed from his palm. The wound zipped itself together like a Ziploc bag. Bridget gaped at his hand, wondering when she'd entered the *Twilight Zone.* The old 50s show would have explained everything, but when he snapped the pocketknife closed, her feelings of unease settled happily into her guts along with reality.

Who is this guy? Why did she feel this overwhelming attraction for him? And why the hell didn't he bleed when cut? No one's skin zipped itself together. If that was the case, there'd be thousands of doctors out of work.

"Who are you?" She shrank from him.

"I told you that before." He causally set the knife aside. "My name is Fredrick MacGregor."

"Okay, then, Mr. Obtuse, maybe a better question should be what are you?"

"You're right. That is a better question." Fredrick offered her a mischievous smile, but showed no teeth. "I'm a Noctivenator, commonly referred to as vampires, one of the Elder Races. What I'm less sure of and far more curious about is what you are."

"Nocti-what?"

"Noctivenitor, currently clanless, but still respected among the Clans." He gave her a sweeping bow straight out of an Errol Flynn movie.

This guy is completely delusional.

"And you, Ms. Shanahan? What are you?"

"What I am is pissed off and wondering where the hell

my clothes are."

Her statement came out more of a snarl than conversation, but he remained unmoved. That just pissed her off more, and she welcomed it. Being mad was preferable to being scared, and right now, the crazy man whose hand didn't bleed scared her spitless.

Plus he thinks he's a vampire.

"Your clothes were ruined by the blood from your wound."

"All of them? My pants, underwear, and socks? I'm not buying it, buster."

He spread his hands. "No, those were merely stained, but it will take some time to get them cleaned."

If her clothes were gone, she'd just scrounge something at hand. Scanning the room beyond his immobile visage, she didn't see anything resembling clothing, but she'd just use the sheet until something better presented itself. Bridget gathered her strength to move but checked herself when someone else came into the room.

"Oh, good, you're awake."

The tall, black-haired woman gave her a friendly smile, but her eyes glittered in the most unusual color of gold in the overhead light. Her movements had the liquid grace of a predator, but when she saw Bridget looking, she smiled gently as she carried a tray laden with a soup bowl, mug, and bread. Bridget's stomach growled with appreciation, but she didn't want to eat here. She needed to get home.

"I can tell you're hungry. I hope you have rested well. Fredrick has been a gentleman, right?"

"I guess that depends on your definition of gentleman." Bridget hadn't meant to be snarky, but it slipped out before she could stop it.

The visitor laughed. "Oh, I like you. I brought you something to eat because it never occurs to him to feed his guests." She shook her head as she set the tray down on the bedside table and shot a glance at the man sitting on the bed. "Have you asked her yet, Fredrick?"

"Asked me what?" Bridget raised her eyebrow. "And where are my clothes?"

"Your jeans and underwear are being washed, but your shirt and bra were stained beyond repair." The dark-haired woman gave her contrite look. "We'll get more for you soon. Until then, you should just rest."

"I am rested, but I really need to get home. Do you have any clothes I can borrow?"

The woman raised her eyebrows and shot a look at Fredrick. "Did you tell her about your visions?" He sighed and shook his head. "Fredrick, what have you been doing up here all this time if not talking to her?"

"I have been talking to her, Cynthia." He took a breath to say more, but Cynthia held up a hand on his protests. "She swears she's human."

"I am human." Bridget clutched the blankets in an attempt to rein in her temper. "He says he's a Nocto, Nocti-whatever. He's crazy."

"Noctivenator."

"Yeah, that. See what I mean?"

Cynthia let her gaze switch between them, her grin getting wider and wider. "She's a good match for you, Fredrick. Strong, determined, and won't take any of your shit."

Despite the oddness of the situation, Bridget laughed. "I do what I can."

Fredrick groaned and shook his head. "Don't encourage her, Cynthia. She's insisting on leaving and she doesn't believe in the Elder Races."

"You have to admit, to the uninitiated it would come across as rather fantastic." Cynthia shrugged. "I'm sure it'll all work out."

"Everyone knows about the Elder Races, at least about werewolves and vampires."

"And they think we're myths, Fredrick. We're safer because of it."

"You think I don't know that?"

It was evidently an old argument, well-worn and comfortable to the combatants. Bridget hoped to use it to her advantage. *Maybe I could say I need the bathroom.* And once she got out in the hallway headed for the door... She tried to think of what she could do without any clothes. The answer came back as "not much".

"I'm sorry to interrupt this fascinating discussion, but is there a chance I can borrow some clothes to get home?"

Fredrick's brows lowered, but Cynthia smiled. "Let's get some food into you first. Healing takes a lot of energy and you'll need your strength." She handed Bridget the tray. "I'm Cynthia Wolfwright, by the way. Fredrick's head of security."

Bridget settled the tray on her lap after making sure the sheet stayed up. "Head of security, eh? Does he have problems with break-ins?"

"Not while I'm around." Cynthia's smile broadened. "He tends to sleep during the day, so he has a few of us to watch out for him."

Bridget snorted. "Even when you turn furry?"

"Especially then." Cynthia grinned widely, and Bridget counted far too many teeth to belong to a human.

She swallowed hard as unease skittered up her spine. *Oh my God, they're sucking me into their delusion.* She glanced down at the food on the tray, but her stomach growled loud enough for the others to hear.

Cynthia chuckled before she nodded to their host. "I'm sure Fredrick will take care of anything you need tonight, but I'll be around in the morning to check in on you. And if he threatens to bite you, just throw cilantro at him."

"Cilantro?"

"Yes. He hates the smell of cilantro. Get some rest and I'll see you in the morning." Cynthia trotted out the door with a wave and a knowing smile.

"See me in the morning?" Bridget coughed through her soup. "No, I need some clothes so I can get home. I can't stay here." She shoved the tray off her lap with a clatter of dishes and sloshing soup. Pain flickered in her side, but its intensity resembled overexertion rather than invasive injury.

"You are in need of rest." Fredrick grabbed her arms and held her steady in the bed. *When did he get up?* His hands were gentle but had the strength of iron bands. "You experienced a traumatic event, and while your body heals quickly, it is still healing. Rest is the necessary component of that."

"I appreciate your concern, but I'm not staying." She leveled her best glare at him. "Look, buddy, I don't know you." *Except when we danced.* "You've kidnapped me to Gloucester, stripped me naked, and claim to be a vampire. All that leads me to think you're considering using me as a meal. In which case, I'm hoping there's a lot of garlic in this soup." She eyed him a moment. "Or cilantro."

"I thought you didn't believe in my 'delusion'." He tilted his head.

"I don't, but you obviously do, and at the moment I have to play by your rules."

Fredrick smiled without showing his teeth, amused. The corners of his mouth curled upwards, and his eyes crinkled at their edges, making her heart flutter.

Damn, why is that so sexy?

"I did consider using you as a meal without your consent, but I find you far too intriguing to feast from without permission." He lowered her back onto the pillows and rescued the bread from the tray, offering it to her. "Here, keep eating. It will help you build your strength."

Strength for what? Did he know she contemplated escape?

She took the bread and considered her next move.

Maybe she didn't need the sheet after all. Of course, once she got out of the house and down the road, she might have a tough time explaining her nakedness, but at least she'd be free. Better to be arrested for indecent exposure than to stay with a madman. There was the small problem of freezing in the cold autumn weather, but she'd worry about that later. She made a show of relaxing and pretended complacency. She could wait. *He has to sleep sometime.* She studied him, her gaze roaming over the visible parts of his body. He met her gaze with a half-smile and a raised eyebrow.

"What are you thinking, Bridget?"

Uhm, what it would be like to sleep with you?

She almost choked on her bread and had to take a sip of water before she could speak.

"Nothing. I'm doing what you asked and eating to recover."

He barked a laugh, a grin lighting up his face. Something about him made him beautiful in a non-traditional way. She liked his eyes the most, with their warm chocolate depths full of secrets, but the dark brows and neatly trimmed black goatee defined his features in a striking way. Her hands ached to stroke the heavy drape of hair falling down his broad, muscular back, and they twitched, almost crushing the bread to crumbs.

"I'll believe that when the Fae return to the world full-time."

And then he says something so weird, I know he's on some sort of medication.

"Right, because along with vampires and werewolves, there are fairies who grant wishes or punish bad bunny foo-foos." She snorted. "Are you sure your nose isn't growing, Pinocchio?"

His jaw clenched as he crossed his arms over his chest. Attraction flared as she took in his rounded pectoral muscles bunching under his shirt.

"The Fae rarely grant wishes, and if they do, they come with steep prices." Fredrick shook his head. "I think you're contemplating something else."

"Well of course I'm contemplating something else. I live in the real world." She rolled her eyes. "I'm thinking about getting home, watering my house plants, and getting on with my life."

With him sitting so close, his natural scent filled her nose. It now reminded her of chocolate truffles with a hint of sea salt. The sweet saltiness had always appealed to her, and she found herself delighting in the scent. *It's too bad he's nuts.*

From what she could see he had a nice home, made a good living, was articulate, and kept himself in decent shape. *At least he's tall enough.* Bridget preferred men who stood taller than her own five-foot-eight inches. Her personality tended to run roughshod over most of the men she'd met, and sent them fleeing for the hills. The exceptions had been the manipulative, abusive bastards her mother tended to favor, and this man.

And he thinks he's a vampire surrounded by werewolves.

No one was perfect. Except for his delusion of vampirism, she might have viewed him as a decent prospect. He didn't seem to be submissive at all. He might be manipulative, but he'd been courteous and attentive.

Bridget frowned, and Fredrick raised an eyebrow.

"Something wrong with the food, Bridget?"

"No, not the food. It's fine. When do you think I could get a ride home?" She set the crumbling bread back on the tray. "I know it's Friday, but I have errands to run and things to do this weekend before the Thanksgiving holiday."

"You need to stay and rest, Bridget. You've taken far more damage than you realize." He gave her a placating smile. "We'll take care of your needs."

Bridget narrowed her eyes. "If you're so hot to take care of my needs, why don't you just take me home? I have all I need there."

He raised his chin and clenched his jaw, and she swore his eyes glowed red for a moment.

There's no such thing as vampires.

She recalled how his hand had zipped itself closed, and doubt encroached on her certainty. Who healed like that in the real world? No one she knew of.

Except if what he said proved to be true she'd joined the group of lightning healing. She slid her hand down her side again without taking her gaze from him. She didn't trust him not to do something if she looked away.

"You need to stay here where you're safe. We don't yet know what all this means."

"All what means?" She dropped her gaze long enough to sneak a peek under the sheet.

Nothing, not even a scar.

Only a purple bruise marred her skin, but it didn't hurt as much as it had a few minutes ago.

This is so weird.

"Why you have nothing but a small bruise left on your side from the mugging."

She snapped her gaze to his face. *Damn, does he read minds?*

She shook her head. "I don't know. It doesn't make any sense."

"Perhaps you've always healed quickly?" He sat down on the chair again, leaning forward on his elbows.

She sat back and shook her head. "No, all the scratches and scrapes I got as a kid healed in the normal way, taking days. Granted, I've never had a bad wound before, but I'd think that would take longer to heal."

"I concur. I did notice you don't have any scars, though. No one heals completely without mark. Why are you unblemished?"

She shrugged. *And how did he notice that?* "My mom taught me to take good care of my skin."

A stab wound was more than just a scratch or scrape, of course, but she'd healed like it was nothing. *Am I a mythical creature?* She snorted with derision.

"There's no way I'm what you say I am, a Nocti-whatever."

"Noctivenator."

"Yeah, that. I enjoy the sun on my face, I think drinking blood is disgusting, and I've never shifted shape into a bat or wolf, full moon or no." About the only thing she did around the full moon was bleed. Every month, on the day. Every time.

"I never said you were a vampire, Bridget. I'm asking you what you are." His brows lowered. "I've never encountered anyone who smells and heals the way you do, and I've been around a long time."

"Right, because you think you're a vampire." She shot him a dry look.

"No, I know I'm a vampire. You think I'm delusional."

"No, I know you're delusional. There's no such thing as vampires."

He started to take a breath to correct her, but she said, "Okay, for the sake of argument, let's say I believe you. But anyone can say they're a vampire, especially with the internet these days. What proof can you give me?"

"Beyond cutting my own hand and showing how it heals?"

Bridget gritted her teeth behind a grimace. "Yeah, beyond that."

Fredrick sighed. "I thought this would be so much easier." He shook his head and shrugged. "I'm sure you studied American history in school, yes?" She nodded. "Then you'd have heard of Jamestown, one of the first European settlements here in the colonies."

"Jamestown, Virginia?"

"That's the one. I was born there in the autumn of the Year of our Lord 1759. I can recall the slaves we owned singing in the fields around our house as they gathered the harvest at the end of summer."

Bridget choked. "Slaves? Your family had slaves?"

"Of course, all landed families did at the time. After the war, it became more prevalent for the Southerners, but it wasn't unheard of in the North."

"War? Which war?"

"For America's Independence. I'm sure you've heard of it. It started around 1776 and ended in 1783 when Britain finally gave up trying to fight the Colonists on their home turf."

"Are you referring to the Revolutionary War?"

"That's the one." He grinned, but still kept his teeth hidden. "I was twenty-four when the war finally ended, and I remember my parents being relieved that I'd survived."

"You fought in the Revolutionary War."

"Yes, with Washington. I even met Paul Revere. Ghastly fellow. Always smelled like burnt silver."

Bridget dropped the sheet from her chest along with her jaw. Paul Revere? The guy who rode, yelling, "The Redcoats are coming! The Redcoats are coming!" That Paul Revere? *No, no, no. This is just a story. Everyone knows of Paul Revere.*

"Has your jaw come unhinged?" Fredrick's question brought her back to the present, but his gaze had latched onto her exposed chest.

She hastily grabbed the green sheet and pulled it over her body with a disgusted grunt.

"It's a pity you should cover those up now that I've had such a marvelous view for the last few seconds."

Bridget's eyes narrowed. "Just because you got a free look doesn't mean it lasts forever, pal. Besides, I thought you were an anatomist. I'm sure you've seen your fair share of breasts over the years."

"Over the *centuries*." His face creased with an irritating smile. "Yes, I have seen many breasts, but rarely have I seen breasts as well-formed as yours."

Why did that statement warm her from the inside? "Uh, thanks, I think." She frowned, trying to get back on track. "All of that is very nice, but not proof. You could find out all that information on Google. To be honest, I don't really want to dispel your delusions, I just want to go home."

Bridget shoved the tray toward him and tried to slide out of the bed, naked or no. She'd raid one of the closets for a coat and walk to the nearest place to call for a taxi. *Maybe I'll just take his trench coat.*

"Bridget, I can't let you leave quite yet." He caught her right arm in a gentle but firm grip. "Not until you tell me what you are."

"You can't let me leave? Or won't?" She pulled against his grip, but it was like being handcuffed to a concrete post. "Who the hell are you to keep me here against my will?"

"The result is the same regardless of semantics. And I'm the one protecting you."

"Protecting me? Buddy, where I'm from, this is called 'kidnapping'." She tugged against his grip again and fear ramped up in her gut. "Why are you keeping me here? Did you escape from a mental institution? Forget to take your meds today? I have got to get out of here!" The last was shouted at him as she jerked her arm to get away. She kept pulling despite the pain in her shoulder as his grip tightened. "*Let me go!*"

She yanked the full weight of her body against his hold on her arm and her shoulder separated. Excruciating pain lanced through her as his fingers bruised her arm, and she whimpered. Fredrick's expression shifted into feral intensity and panic rose to screaming pitch. She pulled harder, trying to breathe through the pain.

Fredrick squeezed her arm until it went numb from the elbow down, the muscles of his jaw clenching while his eyes burned. *Holy shit, he's gonna kill me.* Bridget tried to think of a way to get free, but the pain overwhelmed her brain. *Must get away.* She moaned with each frightful second before she got an idea. Gathering what strength remained, she reversed her momentum and swung her free hand, balled into a fist, at his head. To her amazement, he caught and held it, not crushing her fingers, but holding them tightly closed. She paused, absorbing the meaning of his strength, and realized she'd never get away from him.

He's too strong to fight. It infuriated her she was so easily defeated, and she directed all that impotent rage at him through her livid glare.

"Let. Me. Go."

"You are tired and overwrought. You should rest." He met her gaze unflinchingly. "We will speak more after you've slept."

Fredrick didn't release her until she relaxed her body back into the pillows on the bed. Only the shock of his strength kept her there. If looks could maim, he'd be a writhing mass on the floor. Her eyes burned with the fury, and two tears slowly spilled over her lower lids to drip down her cheeks. She didn't sob, nor did her lips tremble, but her anger seethed beneath her skin. She said nothing, her voice strangled by her wrath.

"Don't try to escape." His voice crackled with cold fury as he stepped back.

What the hell does he have to be mad about?

"I will tell Cynthia and the others to keep an eye and an ear out for you." He raised his chin in warning. "One thing about werewolves and vampires you should know. We are a hundred times faster and stronger than the average human male, so you won't be a problem to catch. I don't recommend trying to run."

She wanted to tell him to fuck off, but the pain in her shoulder cut off her words. Instead, more tears escaped.

He picked up the tray and stepped back from the bed. Bridget said nothing, just stared at him with recrimination. She wouldn't give him the satisfaction of rubbing her numb arm where sensation slowly returned. The pain threatened to make her throw up, but she swallowed against bile. It was badly bruised, maybe even dislocated, but she didn't look at it. She glared as he nonchalantly turned his back on her and strode to the door.

Before Fredrick left, he reached out and grabbed the pocketknife, then switched off the light and shut the door behind him. She lay in the dark with nothing but the bright crack beneath door to illuminate her tears. She'd be damned before she let him keep her. At the soonest possible moment, she'd find a way out.

She waited until his shadow stepped away before she rolled over and allowed herself to cry.

CHAPTER FIVE

Fredrick stepped away and leaned against the wall, careful to keep his shadow from crossing the crack under the door. He closed his eyes and sighed, trying not to hear her sobs or think of the damage he must have done to her arm.

He'd never intended to hurt her or hold her hostage. But when she threatened to leave, his primal heart couldn't let her go, and his hand just kept squeezing. He didn't know why he held her here. Originally his intention was to keep her from harm in Boston, and failing that, to keep her from dying from her wounds.

But she didn't die, and she healed herself without his help.

She's not a vampire or a werewolf.

He shook his head. He could analyze her plasma to find out if she was a carrier of the vampire gene, but he didn't believe she was. Something else about her made her extraordinary and he wanted to know what it was. He shook his head and rubbed his eyes with the heels of his hands. He'd only meant to learn about and protect her.

End of story.

Except the more times he saw her, he wanted to do

more than just protect her. He'd read her sorrow and loneliness in her posture and responses to people. He'd wanted to take away the sadness and scrub the solitude from her life. But he hadn't known her identity until tonight.

Once he recognized her, his attraction for her burned like wildfire, consuming his manners and good sense. *She can't leave. Ever.*

The idea of her escaping him made his stomach clench with fear for the first time since the War of Independence. He couldn't let her go. She belonged to him, his treasure. Her pulling away only excited him like a predator on the hunt with the prey struggling within his grasp, and he'd tightened his grip.

Even if I don't know what she is.

She was far too valuable. Her fury and frustration had smelled like exotic spices, tantalizing him until he damn near drooled. And broke her arm.

Fuck!

Having her naked in the bed had strained his usually iron-like control, and he clenched his hands into fists to keep from storming back into her room and enjoying her glorious curves. He gritted his teeth and shook his head hard, trying to ignore the extension of his canines. Damn, he wanted her in a way he hadn't wanted a woman in decades.

Her feminine beauty flashed through his memory, and his cock hardened joyfully. Her softly rounded belly and those heavy, full breasts called to him like a siren's song. Bridget had a voluptuous and full body, a body meant to be savored and loved. He wanted women with muscle and mass, rather than the skin-covered skeletons often photographed for fashion and porn magazines. Women should look like women with hips, tits, butts, and thighs, not to mention real calves. The gaunt models looked like they stood on swizzle sticks.

His cock started to deflate, and he sighed in relief.
He found Bridget incredibly attractive, and not just her
body. Like the colored lanterns he'd seen in Chinatown in
San Francisco, her eyes sparked green and brown fire, and
she smelled like a fresh stream running through pine-
covered mountains. Her scent shifted to the smell of a
forest fire and rain on dry earth in her anger, an odd
mixture certainly, but no less intoxicating.

His lower anatomy agreed and swelled once more.
Dammit! He almost slammed his fist into the wall, but
restrained himself. She'd hear him and know he stood
outside her room, listening to her cry. *Shit.* He hated it
when women cried. He felt so damn helpless, not a
comfortable sensation for a Noctivenator.

An unearthly snarl escaped from Fredrick's throat, and
he clamped his lips together. He was supposed to save her,
not hurt her. *Way to go, jackass.*

When he'd first gone into Snickerdoodles, he didn't
know who he was looking for, and no one had screamed
"hunted" like his vision had warned. But she'd met his
gaze, and he'd damn near stumbled from the energy rolling
off her. Even other vampires, some older than him by
centuries, didn't have her power. It was a heady mixture of
strength and untapped potential. Intoxicating. Some
masochistic part of him wanted to push her into revealing
her power.

She doesn't even know what she is. Hell, neither did
he, to be honest. He wanted to know more about her,
everything he could, but he'd handled her request to leave
badly.

She didn't request.

Fredrick rubbed his eyes again. It didn't matter. He'd
hurt and infuriated her in his fear of losing her, probably
accelerating her departure.

The mere thought gave him heartburn. *I need her
close.* She was special. He just had to figure out how. Oh,

he knew where she lived, and her scent was etched into his memory. He would always be able to find her. Shanahan, Bridget Erin Diana, born May 18th, 1980.

Her initials spelled BEDS, and that gave him all sorts of ideas.

Down, dammit! She wasn't likely to let him anywhere near her now.

He should go back into her room and apologize for his actions, maybe even explain more why he'd brought her here. But how could he explain she'd filled his visions for the last few days, always with an urgency he'd learned meant danger?

The visions also suggested she'd be important to his life, and his gut recognized the underlying emotional current between them. He'd seen their lifelines woven together through time like Route 66 and Interstate 40 on a U.S. road atlas.

Dear Goddess, please tell me I haven't completely fucked up.

Bridget would never believe him. He suspected she was the practical sort from what little he knew of her. Love at first sight, first mugging, or first bite didn't happen to her. She didn't believe in magic or myths. Hell, she didn't believe in vampires. He could always bite her to show the truth of it, but he'd already pissed her off enough by holding her here.

Fredrick ran a hand over his forehead and eyes, inhaling her scent from them. Goddess of all, she smelled succulent. *At least I didn't tie her to the bed.* The thought of her bound and willing to let him feed off her gave him a raging cockstand. He shoved himself off the wall and stalked downstairs.

I'm so screwed, and not in a good way.

He had to inform his staff Bridget now stayed under duress, but he'd have to get his arousal under control before he faced a room full of werewolves. The lucky critters could smell emotions. He could think of a few times that would've come in handy.

He stopped as if he'd hit an invisible wall at the landing on the stairs. *I've been able to smell Bridget's emotions.* Each one reminded him of weather or natural disasters. If Mother Nature could have emotions, they'd smell like Bridget's. Yet another indication she was important to him.

He grimaced when he thought of what Szilvia would say to that. The Hungarian woman wasn't convinced of his psychic abilities, but tolerated them in hopes time would make him reciprocate her feelings for him. Szilvia loved him and needed him more than he needed her, but his visions told him he'd spend many years with her before they parted ways. *And it's been beneficial.* His gut told him their association would soon come to an end.

He shook his head and made himself continue down the stairs. Nothing to be done about it now. He'd just have to cross that bridge when he came to it.

Fredrick found Szilvia with Matt and a new werewolf named Paul in the kitchen. Matt explained the layout of the estate and the general procedures of Fredrick's household. Matt was Cynthia's right hand man when it came to Fredrick's security, the First in her cadre as Luna to the local werewolf pack.

At least that vision had been beneficial.

Fredrick had hired Cynthia when a vision told him she'd need his help to save her and her loved ones. He'd rescued her mate, Stephen Wolfwright, from being burned alive in a house fire set by a psychotic arsonist, and she'd been devoted to Fredrick ever since. He liked the Wolfwrights, and his connection to them allowed him to live comfortably and safely in a diurnal world.

"How is she?" Matt asked as he paused in his explanation.

"Healthy and angry." Fredrick loaded the dishes into

the dishwasher to distract himself from his furious houseguest. Dishwashers were a godsend for those who hated washing up, though the smell got to him if it wasn't run often enough. "She thinks I kidnapped her. I told her she needed to rest, and if she tried to get out of the house, we'd track her down and bring her back, whether she liked it or not."

"Why did you tell her that, Mr. MacGregor?" Paul asked then blushed and dropped his head when Matt growled at him.

"It's all right, Matt." Fredrick waved at Cynthia's First. "She doesn't have any clothes, and if she took off, she could freeze to death out there. Plus, she's been injured and needs to heal."

"It might be an appealing sight, though." Matt smirked, and Fredrick clamped his teeth together before he bit the werewolf.

"There's still some sort of danger surrounding her, and I won't have her harmed while she's under my care." Fredrick rubbed the back of his neck and frowned.

Szilvia scowled. "Tell us why she's so important again?"

He filled the dishwasher with soap, programmed it for light wash, and closed the door to buy some time. He couldn't tell her Bridget was his life partner based on a gut feeling. Szilvia wouldn't handle the information very well, and at the moment, he wanted only one powerful female angry with him.

It might've been different if I hadn't threatened her.

He grimaced. "I received a vision about her."

"If she doesn't want to stay, Fredrick, you should get rid of her. She's only a She-Meal after all." Szilvia crossed her arms over her chest in challenge.

Anger rose at her disdain, but he shrugged nonchalantly. "Danger threatened her in my vision, and she's in no condition to get home on her own at this point.

So she's staying."

"Oh, for the love of Istvan, just take her to a hotel, leave her a robe, and she'll get home just fine." Szilvia threw her hands up in disgust. "She obviously can heal well enough on her own. Unless you plan to feed on her later?" She raised eloquent eyebrows at him.

He shrugged again, hiding his excitement at the idea of feeding off the fiery-haired woman upstairs. If he wasn't careful, the hard-on he was controlling would break his fly.

He straightened and met Szilvia's gaze. "Are the house accounts up to date? I remember there was a small problem with a recent shipment of the organic coffee beans to Night Caps. Did that get resolved?"

Night Caps was one of his many coffee shops along the East Coast, his favorite, in fact. He was a stickler for making sure his supplies came from organic and environmentally sound farmers and companies. He'd decided if he had to live forever on this earth, he'd better make an effort to take care of it. *I just wish the humans would do the same.*

"Yes, it was discovered that one of our distributors was substituting the organics for the cheaper pesticide grown beans, so we had to drop them."

Szilvia might have other hang-ups, but when it came to business, she didn't fool around with emotional issues.

"It took us a few days, but we managed to find someone who had better scruples and saw to it that everyone knew what our old distributor had done. Last I heard, the poor man went out of business because a fire burned all his warehouses in one go." She was also ruthless as hell.

"As long as we get the organics." Fredrick nodded. "That's the most important thing. Have all the other coffee shops been running well?"

"Well, The Colander and The Last Stand in Rochester had those bacteria outbreaks three weeks ago, but the cleaning crews we sent cleared them up. There have been no other problems. The Boston Tea Party had a rat infestation, but we picked up two cats from the pound, and the problem has gone away. The Cheshire Cat and the Laughing Dog Pub had some illegal workers for a short time, but we got that sorted out by helping them get citizenship. They are family, after all. The Knight Watch had some flooding problems, but…"

Fredrick's attention wavered from her recitation as his thoughts turned back to the unusual woman upstairs. How would he ever apologize for what he'd done to her? Explaining it had all been for her safety after hurting her arm seemed hypocritical.

Damn, he couldn't have been more of an asshole of he tried. *Nothing says generosity and kindness like arm injuries.*

He still didn't know why danger surrounded her. He figured once he'd brought her to his home she'd be safe, but the feeling persisted. He refused to let her go until it faded.

He'd just have to find a way to make it up to her. *Perhaps new clothes, or fine chocolates, or books.* Didn't women who read romance want huge libraries like in that Disney movie about the Beast? He had a library, but it contained mostly scientific texts. *Maybe I could give her a wall for her own books.*

Through his musings, his ears picked up the sounds of footsteps tapping down the staircase, and a door opening and closing quietly. His mind didn't make a connection to its meaning until he realized everyone who should be moving around the house actually stood in the kitchen. His head snapped up and turned toward the front of the house as his body swung into motion before he could actually think of what he was doing.

"Fredrick!" Szilvia's voice cracked at him. "Where are you going?"

****

Bridget bolted out the door into the frigid night and immediately turned right, heading into the trees. She knew she didn't have much time, but if she could hide in the woods or even find a stream to run through so they couldn't use dogs—*or werewolves*—to track her, she'd have a better chance of getting away. She couldn't see any lights from neighbors, so the land around Captain Jerkoff's home had to be either densely wooded or huge. She'd use that to her advantage. Her right arm hung useless, pain jabbing her with each step, but she didn't need it to run.

She worked her way quickly through the trees toward the back of the house, the winter understory snagging at the oversized clothes she'd found. She'd taken her time to dress, listening for anyone outside the bedroom, but her heart thundered loud enough to make it difficult. She'd scrounged a dark hooded sweatshirt that fell to her thighs and some sweatpants she'd had to roll up, but they worked well enough to get her out of the house. She thanked God someone had left her shoes next to the bed.

She pushed her legs faster, trying to get as far away from any structures as possible. She heard doors open behind her and voices shouting orders.

Damn. That didn't take long.

Bridget tightened her lips and focused on moving forward as fast and as quietly as she could. She wouldn't let anyone keep her as a pet.

The scent of the air changed from damp woodlands to icy water, and she picked up sounds of the river ahead of her. The voices behind her had gone silent, and she hoped they'd lost her trail as she veered toward the river bank. Maybe she could work her way along the river's edge and find another residence or some sort of civilization where she could get help.

Didn't it just figure? The sexiest guy she'd ever met with enough wealth to own a huge, beautiful house had to be a raving lunatic who thought he needed a liquid diet. Why couldn't the sexy guy who wanted her just be normal, friendly, and reasonable?

She hated to admit it, but Fredrick had frightened and infuriated her. Hell, he'd hurt her. Screaming pain blazed through her every time she even thought of moving her right arm. She couldn't get away from his delusions of vampirism soon enough. He seemed stronger than an average guy, but he probably worked out at a gym. And she'd been scared. Fear made her body go weak and watery.

That's my story and I'm stickin' to it.

Her thoughts splintered when she caught motion out of the corner of her eye. She didn't stop running, but she focused her gaze on the place she'd seen movement. Nothing showed, but she pushed her body faster and listened hard. Panic crept up her throat, but she swallowed against the building shriek.

Gotta make it to the river. Gotta make it to the river.

She couldn't hear anything over the thunder of her own heart, but the scents of spiced apples and burned rubber seared her nose just before something hard tackled her. Her shriek erupted as she toppled to the ground and panic exploded. She struggled hard and fresh pain hit her as her injured arm snapped back into its socket with a meaty pop.

Holy fuck! The pain left her breathless and she collapsed, but it didn't matter with the large, dark, and heavy weight on top of her.

The weight turned its head, and two red, glowing eyes glared back at her. Harsh breathing warmed her face and neck while panic rebuilt her shriek. Her own panting competed with his, and they sounded like they practiced *Pranayama* in some high-end yoga studio. Anger surged as she squirmed to get away.

"Get off me!"

"I told you not to run." His grip tightened with his growl. "I told you we'd catch you. You were injured and needed to rest. This isn't a joke. You shouldn't be out here in the dark."

"No, it isn't a joke, and I don't want to stay with you." Bridget struggled in his grip. "Let me go. You can't keep me here."

"I beg to differ." He hauled her to her feet and held her fast. Bitter experience kept her from pulling away.

Gotta get away.

She relaxed all her muscles and let gravity have at her. Her body slithered out of his arms to the ground.

"What the—"

As soon as she was free, she scrambled to her feet and bolted away from him. He cursed and grabbed for her, but she ducked and twisted out of reach. She managed to dodge trees and underbrush as she scanned the dark forest. She darted to her left around a tree to give herself a little cover, but the New England woods had far less underbrush than those in Michigan where she'd grown up.

Maybe I can—

She didn't get to finish her thought as Fredrick caught her again. This time, he lifted her off her feet and threw her kicking and snarling over his shoulder.

"Oh my God, let me go!" Bridget rained blows on his backside with her good arm, twisting her body off of his shoulder, and trying to slam her knees into his gut. He merely tightened his arms around her knees and hips, ignoring her hands entirely. Her fury mounted, and she opened her mouth to bite him through his mock turtleneck sweater.

His snarl echoed through the silent trees as he lugged her back to the house. "Do that, and I'll show you what biting really is."

She stiffened at the cold menace in his voice then

slumped against his back. Her arm was still sore, and her torso hurt from the impact with the hard ground. Each step he took jabbed his shoulder into her belly, and her stomach roiled.

It'd serve him right if I threw up down his back.

Cold, pain, frustration, and defeat flashed through her in a kaleidoscope of sensations. She pressed her face against his shoulder blade and let the tears loose. The heat of his body seeped into her and the delicious scent of his clothes filled her nose, but the fear wouldn't let her enjoy them. She turned her head to rest her cheek on his back and closed her eyes. Tears oozed out from under her lids and she sobbed. God only knew what he'd do with her now.

He said nothing as he hauled her back to the house. Only the crack of his footsteps and her hiccupping sobs broke the angry silence between them. Bridget opened her eyes as they stomped through the kitchen past two surprised young men.

She took a breath to demand help, but Fredrick left the room too swiftly, bouncing her uncomfortably against his shoulder. He jogged up the stairs and back into the room she'd left a few minutes before. Despite his evident anger, he deposited her gently in the bed, catching her head to keep her from cracking it on the headboard.

Fury boiled beneath her skin as tears continued to flow, but she just lay there without moving as he pulled her shoes off. He reached for her sweatshirt, but she hissed at him and he paused. His own fury lay reflected on his expression, but he said nothing as he lifted the covers and slid her legs under them.

Now what, asshole? She raised her chin in challenge despite her tears. She wouldn't make it easy for him.

At last, he retreated to the door, only pausing to flick off the light. Then he stepped out into the hall and closed it behind him. When he'd gone, the tears renewed their onslaught of her cheeks, and her mind ridiculed her as a big baby. Her shoulder hurt, her ribs ached, and she had scratched one palm when she landed on the ground. She rolled onto her left side away from the door, and let her dirty tears soak the expensive pillowcase. *Take that, Asshole MacGregor.*

Sobs marked the seconds and minutes in untold numbers before she heard the door open, and someone came in. The person didn't turn on the light, and she kept her back resolutely to the door. She didn't care who it was. They wouldn't help her anyway.

Surprise zinged through her when something thumped on the bedside table, and a weight settled onto the bed.

"I've brought you some *Arnica montana* and some water. You are going to hurt terribly tomorrow with that arm." Fredrick paused as if waiting for a response.

Oh yeah? Why do you think that is? She didn't dare voice her fury in case he had something horrible in mind for her. *It puts the lotion on its body or it gets the hose.*

He sighed. "The *Arnica* will help with the pain. I suggest you take six pellets and let them dissolve under your tongue." He paused again.

Does he really think I'm going to answer? She refused to give him the pleasure.

"Good night, Bridget."

Fuck you. I'd have a good night if you'd let me go, asshole!

His weight lifted from the bed, and she heard the door open and close one more time. She growled and closed her eyes, wishing she could punch her pillow.

She had no intention of taking anything he gave her. God knew what kind of poison or drug he'd offered. *Arnica montana?* What kind of medicine was that? He could keep his little date-rape drug to himself. Hell, she wouldn't even take aspirin from him.

Groaning with anger and frustration, she tried to find a comfortable position for her aching body.

CHAPTER SIX

Fredrick roared and attacked the granite sparring dummy with fresh fury. The memory of Bridget's foray into the winter-frosted woods made his blood boil. Each one of her tears burned his back as he'd hauled her back to the house, fresh pain and sorrow staining his spirit. Every sob etched new wounds into his heart.

He threw more effort into the strikes he made on the dummy, the crack of bamboo sharp in the silence of the gym. The impacts diminished none of his rage despite his efforts.

He hadn't wanted to hurt or frighten her, but he'd done both. It didn't matter that he knew she was in danger. To her, he seemed like a deranged lunatic. Fredrick twirled and slammed the staff into the head of the dummy.

The staff splintered and spun away in ragged pieces, crashing into the far corners of the room. Fredrick bent over with his hands on his knees, trying to breathe through the fury. In through his nose, out through his mouth as his meditation teacher had instructed. With his blood pounding in his ears, he couldn't hear much, but he scented his visitor the moment the door closed.

"Looks like you have a little cleaning to do."

"Just be glad you don't have to do it. What are you doing here, Stephen?" Fredrick straightened and tossed the broken end of the staff away from him. "I thought you were home with Cynthia."

Cynthia's husband leaned his hip against a rack of weights and crossed his arms over his chest. "Matt called Cynthia when he heard you going crazy down here. She wasn't available." Stephen winked with smug satisfaction. "So I thought I'd stop by and see if there was anything I could do."

Fredrick snarled as he swung back to the rack holding other staffs. "There's nothing you can do about my stupidity."

The Alpha of the Essex County Pack snorted ruefully. "Yeah, that's up to each of us. Wanna talk about it?"

Fredrick took his stance in front of the dummy. "No."

"All right." Stephen raised his hands in a show of surrender. "It's your call, but you better not take it out on Cynthia or the wolves because I'll be back to hash it out with you then."

Fredrick snarled. "It's a woman."

Stephen laughed. "Isn't it always?"

Fredrick clobbered the granite dummy with six hard and fast strokes, but it didn't alleviate his frustration.

"Which woman is this and why does she matter in the grand scheme of things?"

Fredrick sighed and dropped his guard. "She's the woman upstairs that I'm holding hostage because I know she's special in some way."

"Holding hostage?" Stephen raised his eyebrows. "How's that working out for you?"

"Not well." Fredrick scowled. "She's in danger—my gut's screaming it. But the only way I can think of to keep her safe is to keep her here."

"And she doesn't want to stay."

"No." Fredrick stared at the butt of the staff planted

between his feet. "She tried to escape, but I caught her and brought her back."

Stephen nodded. "That's not too bad."

"Maybe, if I hadn't dislocated her shoulder first and then locked her in."

"Oh, boy. Yeah, that won't be winning you any points." Stephen shook his head. "How old are you again? Don't you know anything about wooing women?"

"Evidently not." Fredrick rubbed his forehead, mentally kicking himself for his treatment of Bridget. "She scared me. Tired, injured, and in need of healing, she wouldn't make it off the estate, much less the few miles to Gloucester's downtown."

"Maybe, but even with all that, it sounds like she at least figured out how to get out of the house and make a run for it."

Why does he sound so impressed? And why do I agree? Fredrick had to admit he admired Bridget's fortitude and determination. She might believe he was crazy, but she still took the chance she could get away from him. *Goddess, she must think I'm going to really hurt her now.*

"Have you just tried talking to her?"

Fredrick growled. "Of course I have."

"And?" Stephen waved for him to elaborate.

"And she thinks I'm crazy and doesn't believe in the Elder Races at all."

"But she's human, right? That makes sense."

"Except she's not human. She's something else, something I've never met."

Stephen bit his bottom lip and rubbed his chin in consideration. "Goblin? Dragon?"

Fredrick shook his head. "I don't think so."

"*Morukai?*"

"I—" Fredrick stopped himself.

Could she be one of the fabled shamans of the

Goddess? He'd only ever met one in his whole life when his mother offered him as a true disciple of the Goddess. A *Morukai* Priestess blessed him and told him he was meant for great things in time. At the age of ten he hadn't paid too close attention, though he remained devout all his life.

The *Morukai* were the one Elder Race most like a chameleon. They could be anyone or anything, blending perfectly into the people with whom they lived.

"She might be *Morukai*." He sighed. "Hell, I don't know. And I don't think she knows, either. She didn't know she could heal as quickly as she does and she knew nothing of the other Elder Races."

Stephen shrugged. "Would the *Morukai* who live with humans know about the other Elder Races? I don't know. It'd make sense that they would, but maybe not." He waved it away as irrelevant. "But either way you need to go up and apologize to her."

"Yes, you're right."

"Hey, being married to a queen bitch werewolf has taught me a lot about women." Stephen smirked. "Let me tell you, being literally in the doghouse is not fun at all, especially when she can hear and smell you coming. Talk to her, make amends for hurting her, and see if you can figure this out with her. I bet she's not keeping secrets from you so much as she doesn't have all the information either."

Fredrick nodded, taking the staff back to the rack before he grabbed a towel to mop up the sweat off his neck and face. It gave him a few moments to think on what Stephen had said. Talking hadn't worked the first time, but he'd been operating on the premise that she knew what she was. Maybe if he sat with Bridget and worked through what they both thought they knew, they could come to an understanding.

He shot a look at the clock and grimaced. Three A.M. wasn't the best time to have a heart-to-heart.

"You have a good point, Stephen. But I'll wait until she's rested. No point in irritating her more tonight."

Stephen snorted, but didn't gainsay Fredrick.

"Probably not. You gonna be okay now?"

"Yes, thank you. Sorry to interrupt your evening."

"Oh, it's okay. I needed to give Cynthia time to recover." He winked and Fredrick resisted the urge to strangle him. "I'll tell her everything's good with you. Just do me a favor and talk to your woman. Believe me, it'll make things easier in the long run."

The Alpha werewolf clapped him on the shoulder before taking his leave. Fredrick rubbed his face and neck with the towel again, not because he needed it, but because it gave him time to think out his plan. And he'd need a good one to face Bridget again.

****

Bridget woke to more pain than she'd ever experienced in her life. Stiffness solidified her right shoulder into immobility, and her ribs felt like the idiot with the baseball bat had returned to finish the job he'd started on her left side.

The scratch in her hand throbbed with her heartbeat, and a spreading bruise in the shape of a handprint marred the skin of her right bicep. The only thing good about waking up was the opulent bed beneath her ass. By the pale light seeping in the window, she judged the sun had been up for a while.

Groaning, she slowly turned over to look around and found the glass of water and a little blue plastic tube on the bedside table. Fredrick's little date-rape drug.

No deal, jackass.

She knew she had to get up and move before her body atrophied into the fetal position, but dread threaded through her mind. Pain hovered at the edge of her awareness, waiting to pounce when she stretched. It would spike every muscle she had and probably a few more she didn't even know about.

Walk. All I have to do is walk a little around the room, and it'll be better.

Moving gingerly, Bridget slid her feet toward the edge of the bed and pushed off with her left arm. She gritted her teeth and hissed when her feet touched the floor, each muscle protesting. Walking would be a bitch. Taking a deep breath, she forced herself to stand.

Sweet glory of the second coming.

Apparently, holding herself upright used muscles pulverized by the psychotic locomotive who'd tackled her the night before. Everything from her hips to her shoulders protested their use, even her boobs. *What the hell? My boobs didn't do anything.*

Taking a deep breath, she forced herself to step cautiously away from the bed. Each step dragged an involuntary moan from her lips as her toes dug into the plush carpet. She tried to focus on reaching her goal silently, but by the time she made it to the window, she gasped, breathless. She leaned her face against the cold glass, trying to catch her wind.

Damn. Definitely not "good pain".

Bridget let the cool of the window distract her. Outside, rain pelted the grounds in silver streaks. She shivered, glad she was inside. *Yeah, in a gilded prison.* She scanned the world outside, taking in the location of her window and the distance from the ground. She appeared to be on the second floor above an Asian style patio cover. The wood gleamed dimly in the faded light. If she hung from the window sill outside, her feet would be no more than a couple of feet from the roof of the cover.

Yeah, if my body didn't hurt like a bitch.

She slowly stretched her sides and back, breathing through the protests of the muscles. She tried to raise her right arm above her head, but pain screamed across her awareness, burning a path from her neck all the way down to her wrist.

"I won't be using that arm much," she grumbled, her breath painting opaque circles against the cold glass.

"You talk to yourself like that, and people will start to think you're crazy."

Bridget whipped her head around and stared at the doorway. A pale, white blonde woman stood there holding another tray and examined Bridget with her cold silver-blue eyes. She had a pleasant body with small, round breasts and generous hips much like Bridget's own, but her sharp, angular features and thin lips gave her a sour expression. At the moment, an unfriendly smirk creased her mouth.

"Thanks for the tip." Bridget raised her chin. "Who are you?"

"You can call me Miss Vértolvaj."

"Verto Vawdge?"

"Vértolvaj.". The woman stalked in the room and set the tray down on the other bedside table with a disdainful flick of her head. "I see you haven't drunk any water or taken the medicine Mr. MacGregor offered. I simply can't imagine why he'd make all this effort for you since you're really nothing more than a good fuck and a meal, but that's his business, I suppose. Even if you are ungrateful."

Bridget gaped at Miss Snootypants. *What the hell was that about being a 'good fuck and a meal'?* Two could play the rudeness game.

"I take it you think you're a vampire, too?"

"Well, of course I am."

The woman smiled broadly, the wan light glinting off elongated canine teeth filed into points. *Good glory, these people are completely unhinged.* Bridget gripped the windowsill behind her to hide her unease and rolled her eyes.

"I thought vampires couldn't stand to be out in the

daylight." She raised her eyebrows in her best dubious expression. What was that wannabe vamp group she'd heard of in college? Jeez, they were all nuts.

"A myth, not that you'd know the difference anyway."

"Are you always this rude, or are you just making an effort on my behalf?" Bridget had the pleasure of watching surprise bloom on the other woman's face. "Because I was kidnapped, not that you'd know the difference. Let me fill you in. It wasn't my choice to be here and I tried to leave last night. So if you want me gone so badly, why don't you just go back to *Mr. MacGregor* and convince him to let me go, 'cause I'll do it happily."

"I'd be happy to inform Mr. MacGregor of your wishes as soon as he rises."

"Rises, right. Like the sun." Bridget flashed a false grin. "When will that be? Dusk? Sunset? Give Mr. Sunshine a message for me, won't you? Tell him kidnapping is a felony."

She turned her back on the other woman and tried to rein in her frustration. The weather matched her mood and the pain spurred her anger. *Can't leave and can't escape.*

An offended hiss snaked through the air, and the door slammed shut behind the woman's stomping heels. Bridget smiled until she heard the bolt slide home and realized the crazy bitch had locked her in.

She hobbled from the window to the door, her muscles screaming in protest as her fury mounted. It didn't help that she tried the knob. *It's locked, you idiot.* It rattled, but refused to turn. She wanted to pound against the wooden barrier and raise hell about being held hostage, but she didn't have the strength to beat through the pain. *And what am I going to do? They proved last night they can outrun me.*

"Fuck! God dammit! Mother pussbucket!"

Bridget turned her back to the door and leaned against it, trying to figure out what to do next. Exhaustion nagged at her body like lactic acid, burning through the small reserve of energy she'd built by sleeping.

Maybe I can go out the window. If she was quiet enough, they wouldn't know she was gone until too late. But pushing off the door made her body scream in protest. *Yeah, I probably can't even open the window, much less climb out.*

Somehow, she had to find the strength to get back to the bed. Her stomach grumbled in commiseration as she continued to shuffle across the floor. Another moaning journey brought her to the bedside, exhausted and aching. She leaned against the mattress to catch her breath before she could even decipher what the tray held. Her mind identified cheese, crackers, grapes, cherry tomatoes, sliced summer sausage, and a shelled hardboiled egg beside another glass of water and a folded napkin.

They folded the napkin? Since when do kidnappers have manners?

The only thing missing was silverware. She barked a humorless laugh. At least they'd cut everything into bite-sized pieces for her.

This is just unreal. I'm locked in, but they thoughtfully cut my food for me.

Bridget braced her pelvis against the tall bed and reached for the plate of food. Her hand shook so much she knocked the water glass off the tray, sending a crystalline arc of liquid onto the carpet. She cursed as the glass bounced and rolled a few feet away, leaving a wet trail behind it. She dropped to her knees to crawl after it, but the muscles protested so much she sat on her butt and rested a moment, glaring at the glass.

Smooth move, stupid. Now how are you going to get back up, much less on the bed?

She tried to get her legs under her, but everything hurt too much. She paused, trying to breathe through the pain and coax the strength back into her limbs.

But the longer she sat, the harder it was to move. Eventually, she gave up and fell to her side, groaning. Reaching out with her left arm, she made one last attempt to pull her weight up, but she didn't have the strength. *Shit.* Anger and frustration overflowed her eyes in tears. She laid her head on the floor and let loose all her emotions, including her hunger. Exhaustion washed over her, and she sniffled her way to sleep, trying to ignore the scents of dust and dirt in the carpet beyond her nose.

****

Dusk came early and Fredrick dragged his ass out of sleep with a new sense of purpose. He had to make Bridget understand why he'd brought her to his house. He'd spent the rest of the night after talking to Stephen sorting his words and explanations with the meticulous efforts of a scientist. He wanted his arguments to have clarity and references.

Unfortunately, everything he had to tell her sounded as fantastical as an adventure novel. She didn't believe in the Elder Races, though he could prove they existed, and she'd swear she was human.

And she's not that.

What could she be?

There is more to Heaven and Earth than is dreamt of in your philosophy, Horatio.

Truer words were never written. Fredrick frowned as he stopped at the top of the stairs. His library contained several manuscripts of records kept on the Elder Races of this world. He knew because his uncle, Drake MacGregor, lived in Three Lakes, Michigan as the town Archivist.

He shot a look at the door where he'd kept Bridget, but diverted his strides down the stairs to his library office. The evening dusk filled the room with darker shadows especially with the rain still sheeting down. Despite the gloom, calm and comfort surrounded him as he switched on the overhead lighting.

He checked the time and picked up the phone. *Six-thirty. Still early.* He dialed the number and settled into his comfortable desk chair.

"This is Drake."

"Uncle Drake, how are you this evening?"

"Fredrick? Good to hear from you. To what do I owe the honor?" Drake sounded genuinely pleased.

"I was hoping you can help me with some research." Fredrick rubbed his jaw as he thought out the words he wanted. "I've met someone—"

"Someone? A special someone of the female persuasion?" Drake's voice held interest so sharp Fredrick could almost smell it through the phone.

"Yes, and yes, but not in the way you surmise." Fredrick laughed. "I've met a woman I've been having visions about. She was in danger, still is as far as my gut tells me, but she's not as human as she or I thought."

"Wait, back up a bit here. What do you mean, 'as she thought'? Is she more than human?" He could almost see Drake waving his hands.

"Yes."

"And she was unaware of it? How did you both find out differently?"

Fredrick sighed and rubbed the bridge of his nose. "She got mugged and stabbed."

"What? She was in danger and you let her get mugged and stabbed? Fredrick, I taught you better than that."

"I know, I know. I killed him and drained him if that makes any difference." He grimaced at the weakness of his excuse. "But it turns out she didn't really need my help. She can heal as fast as the Elder Races, but she's not Noctivenatori or werewolf, or anything else I've encountered."

"What do you think I can do to help?"

"I was hoping you could tell me a little about all the Elder Races you know and maybe I'd get a clue to her species."

Drake sighed. "Can you at least narrow it down for me by telling me where she's from or who her parents were?"

"No, I don't know anything other than she's a redhead, lives in Boston, and was born on May 18th, 1980."

"Hmm." The sound of rustling papers came from Drake's end of the call. "Can you tell me what she smells like? Anything would be better than generalities."

"Smells like? How would that help?"

"Each species has a scent. You know this. Most of the Noctivenatori have a musk that's fairly metallic from their blood diet. Some of the worst of them smell like wet dirt or mold." Drake huffed. "Not pleasant. Does she smell like a werewolf or something more rare, like a goblin or dragon?"

"Dragons exist?" Fredrick snorted. "I thought they were myths, like unicorns."

"Yes, dragons exist." A curious tension filled Drake's voice, but he went on before Fredrick could ask about it. "Have you noticed her scent? Did anything jump out at you?"

Fredrick sighed and searched his memory. "Yes, I've been able to smell her emotions, a lot like werewolves say they can."

"Really? That's unusual. What did they smell like?"

"Natural things like pine forests in the rain, or a snow storm or a forest fire. Things like weather or natural events."

More papers rustled in the background. "Wait. Which day did you say she was born?"

Fredrick frowned at the phone. "May 18th 1980. Why?"

"Oh, oh, oh. Sweet Goddess of all. That's the day Mount St. Helens erupted in Washington State."

"So?"

"So, I have an old text here that talks about the Goddess taking physical form."

"Physical form. Like the *Morukai* shamans?"

"No, something more, something like an Avatar, an incarnation of the Goddess here in this world." Drake grew silent for a few moments. "It says here that the Goddess will take physical form to give Her Elder Races a little extra umph to protect and guide, particularly during times of darkness and distress."

Fredrick sat up. "I wasn't aware it was a time of darkness or distress."

"You've heard of the Sword of God, correct?"

A chill ran down his spine. "The fanatical religious group of assassins who hate everything not human?"

"Yes, they were very active in this country at the Salem Witch Trials, killing off as many of the Elder Races as they could under the guise of witchcraft." Drake paused. "Perhaps they've become more active now."

"And you think Bridget is the Goddess's Avatar?"

"Oh, Bridget, is it?" Drake chuckled. "I think it's a possibility you might want to consider. Especially given your mother's proclivity for worshiping the Goddess."

Fredrick couldn't argue. His mother had inducted him into the faith of the Goddess when he was a child, even going so far as to have him blessed by a *Morukai* Priestess.

"How often does the Avatar appear?"

Drake sighed. "It isn't clear. It's not something we can predict, apparently. But here's the thing. The Avatar almost always shows up the same time as a large eruption of a volcano."

"Come on, a volcano? Kilauea has been erupting for decades."

"And how many Hawaiians say they've met Pele?" Drake chuckled. "But I'm talking about big eruptions that take out cities and towns. Pompeii was one. Mount

Mozama that created Crater Lake was another. Valles Caldera in what's now New Mexico. And Mount St. Helens in 1980."

Fredrick sat back and let his gaze unfocus. There were a lot of clues to suggest Drake's assertion was correct, but only Bridget could tell him for sure. *And she doesn't seem to know.* He rubbed a hand over his face. If she was indeed the Avatar, he'd better apologize for being such an ass soon, or it could go badly for him.

"I don't know, Drake. It seems a bit far-fetched."

"You don't believe?"

"This could've been an accident of happy coincidences."

"I don't think the word 'happy' belongs here. Besides, why would you have gotten the visions of her in danger if she wasn't someone so important to you?" Drake snorted into the phone. "Rescuing damsels in distress isn't your style, Fredrick, not even when you were young."

Fredrick groaned. "I know. Thanks for the research, Uncle Drake. I'll see what else I can find out from here."

"Do you even know what danger she's in?"

"No, but the feeling persists even after I brought her here."

Drake hissed. "Watch your back and hers, Fredrick. If the warnings continue, you're not safe yet."

"I know. Thanks again, Uncle Drake."

"Take care."

Fredrick clicked off the phone and listened to the rain drum against the windows as his thoughts sifted through Drake's suggestions. If she truly was the Avatar, he needed to do some serious groveling. If not, he still needed to make sure she remained safe.

But who else could she be?

He scrubbed his face with his hands and shook his head, brushing the last few strands of his hair out of his face. *I better go check on her.* He rose and returned to the bedrooms upstairs, his gut tightening the closer he got to her room.

Would she scream at him or damn him with those fierce eyes? She had made an attempt to run and he suspected only her injuries kept her inside the house at the moment. Of course, given her healing abilities, he was surprised she hadn't tried again. But no one had left notes or messages about a second attempt while he slept.

He paused at her bedroom door, trying to gather his thoughts and wits. *I can do this and make it right.* He took a deep breath and turned the knob.

Except the door wouldn't open.

What the hell? Why is the door locked?

Maybe Bridget had made another attempt to get out again. But someone would've told him about it in a note or text. He frowned as he turned the key in the lock. Who would lock her in?

Fredrick found Bridget asleep in an undignified heap on the floor beside the bed. *What is she doing on the floor?* The scents of anger, desperation and wet carpet assaulted his nose as he gently picked her up and laid her in the bed. Tear stains and a stubble pattern etched the skin of her cheek as he tucked the covers around her.

Another scent, faded and dilute, hovered at the edge of his recognition, but the other scents overwhelmed his nose. He shook his head. Something wasn't right.

He frowned at the empty glass a few feet from the bed. The food remained untouched, but a water stain streaked the carpet. What had she been doing? Throwing the glass?

He retrieved the cut crystal and replaced it on the tray, then stood looking at his unwilling guest. He wanted explain to her why she had to stay, but he didn't want to wake her up. She looked exhausted.

Are you the Avatar of the Goddess, Bridget? He settled himself beside her on the bed, studying her features.

When not angry, she had a serenity he'd only seen on

statues found in cathedrals and temples. Sadness etched the corners of her mouth and he wanted to erase it, making the lines on her face be those of laughter and joy. Unfortunately, each time he insisted on protecting her, her fury erupted much like Drake's volcanoes.

Fredrick sighed. She hadn't touched the food, but surely she'd been hungry. Given the amount of energy it took to heal, he'd thought she'd be ravenous. Maybe she preferred only fruit and vegetables.

He groaned and shook his head at his clumsy attempts to make her comfortable. He knew so little about her, but at least now he had a clue to research. He should start by getting her some suitable clothing beyond the sweatshirt and sweatpants. *Maybe a warm Cashmere sweater and jeans.* He'd have to ask Cynthia what size Bridget wore. He'd also have to make sure she wasn't locked in again. As much as it was a pain to chase her down, he'd much rather give her the choice.

Before he could stop himself, he reached out and stroked Bridget's cheek with the backs of his fingers. Her skin felt like velvet, and she sighed a little wistfully at his touch. At least, that was what he told himself.

"It will be better, I promise, Bridget. Just trust me, please," he whispered. "We'll figure this out together."

She frowned a little but didn't wake, and he retreated before she discovered him at her bedside. He'd bring her another tray with a new glass of water and a plate of fruits and vegetables in hopes she'd prefer them to the meat.

Fredrick paused at the door. He wanted to touch her again, to reassure himself she wasn't a figment of his visions, but he forced himself to leave the room and the deliciously-scented woman in it. Once the danger surrounding her abated, he'd court her regard properly. He wanted more time with her to learn who she truly was. But until then, he'd do his utmost to protect her, even if it meant enraging her.

CHAPTER SEVEN

Bridget woke to complete darkness with a vague memory of spiced apples and gentle hands. Turning her head to scan the room, she struggled to understand where she was and how much time had passed. Frowning, she tried to remember why being in the bed felt so strange.

Wait a minute. I was on the floor.

Sitting up, she reached out to switch on the bedside light. Squinting against the sudden glare, Bridget found the tray laden with fresh fruit and veggies, and a new glass of water. Someone had brought her new food.

Couldn't have been Ms. White Bitch. She would've kicked me before she helped me.

Bridget shook her head and drank the water to ease the dryness of her throat. Her hands no longer shook from fatigue or stiffness, and she could sit up with ease. Her right arm still twinged, and her ribs ached a little, but not as badly as when she'd shuffled across the floor. The only real discomfort came from her stomach, reminding her she hadn't treated it well.

Not my fault.

She finished the water and scanned the room for anything else new. A little blue plastic tube stood up right next to the plate. Curious, she picked it up and read the small print carefully.

arnica montana

HOMEOPATHIC MEDICINE

ACTIVE INGREDIENT: listed above. **USE:** for self-limiting condition listed below or as directed by a physician.

WARNING: DO NOT USE if pellet dispenser seal is broken.

There were other warnings, but she skipped them to read what it was supposed to treat.

TRAUMA, BRUISES, MUSCLE SORENESS

Been there, done that.

She shook the tube and listened to the rattle of the pellets inside. *Maybe he's hoping it'll keep me drugged and compliant.* But the seal remained unbroken, and the tube looked official. Of course, given the décor of the house she'd seen on her way out, Mr. MacGregor and company had enough money to make anything for their own purposes.

Breaking the seal, she sniffed at the contents, but nothing came to her nose. She rattled the tube again and considered her options.

Possibility one, she could experience pain relief and rest. Possibility two, she could be pliant and submissive to whatever he chose to do to her. But he could've done that while she slept if he wanted her out of it.

She took a moment to concentrate on her body. Nothing hurt beyond the aches and pains she sustained during her getaway attempt. He hadn't touched her that she could tell. She still wore the clothes she'd scrounged and they didn't appear torn.

So not sexually assaulted. That's a plus. But she remained stuck in this house with people who were under some fantastical delusion. At least, she hoped they were delusional. She thought she'd seen a red glow in Fredrick's eyes a time or two, but it could've been a trick of the light and a severe lack of oxygen to her brain.

Or he could be telling the truth.

Bridget debated for a while until she heard a gentle knock at the door. *They're knocking now? That's rich considering they locked me in.* Shaking her head, she leaned back and closed her eyes. She supposed she could tell whoever it was to go away, but if she truly wanted to get out of this place she needed the door unlocked. The memory of the deadbolt sliding home made her shiver.

"May I come in?"

Bridget opened her eyes to see Cynthia hesitating on the threshold. The black haired woman held some clothing folded neatly into a compact pile.

"Like I could stop you."

Cynthia grimaced. "This is true, but I've found it works better to be polite."

Bridget shrugged with one shoulder.

"How are you feeling?" Cynthia crossed the room, setting the clothing down on the bed. "You haven't touched any of your food. Aren't you hungry?"

Bridget shot her a dry look. "Hungry? Yes. Trust your food? No."

"Do you think it's poisoned?"

"Poisoned?" Good God, she hadn't even considered that, but it made sense. "Why would I think anything like that? It isn't as if you've held me here against my will or locked me in or anything. Oh, wait. You did, didn't you?"

"I heard that you left the house last night." Cynthia continued as if Bridget hadn't spoken at all. "I'm impressed. I can't imagine you were feeling very well after what happened to you in Boston. I guess we underestimated you."

"Is that why you locked me in here?"

"What are you talking about?"

"The door. Didn't you notice it was locked?"

Cynthia shook her head. "It wasn't locked."

Bridget blinked before anger welled into her chest. "Yes, it was. The woman with white hair locked it on the way out yesterday."

Cynthia nodded slowly. "So that's what the note was about." She sighed. "Fredrick left a note for me to find some clothing that would fit you and that you had the run of the house as long as you didn't leave it. I didn't know why he needed the last bit until now."

"So the door won't be locked from now on?"

"No. We have no need to keep you locked in. We can catch you fairly easily if we need to."

This woman's insane.

Bridget snorted. "Are you suggesting I buy into this delusion about werewolves and vampires?"

Cynthia sighed. "Unfortunately for you, it's not a delusion. However, I can guarantee the food is fresh, organic and safe. I'd be able to smell anything in it."

"You sound like you expect me to believe you, but you're one of my captors. Hard to believe someone who won't let me leave."

Cynthia laughed. "You're right. I wouldn't believe me, either, with that perspective. But I give you my word as a woman and a Luna that the food is safe and will help you replenish the energy you've used in healing."

Bridget narrowed her eyes. "What's a Luna?"

Cynthia cocked her head like a curious dog. "Tell you what. I'll trade you that information for you telling me who you are."

Bridget groaned and shook her head. "I don't understand what the big deal is. My name is Bridget Shanahan, and I'm a project manager for a company in Boston."

"That's just your cover story to hide among the humans. I want to know who you really are."

"Cover story? For what?"

"You really don't know, do you?"

Bridget could only gape at her. They seemed to believe she held some grand secret from them, but as far as she knew, she was human. Had been from birth.

Cynthia looked at her a moment with consideration, then tilted her head back and took a deep breath in through her nose. "You smell like an autumn pine forest with the bitter tang of frustration for flavor. Humans don't normally smell like that. In fact, they usually smell like raging pheromones, sweat, fear, and primate." She bit her bottom lip with an especially sharp looking tooth. "You don't know you're not completely human."

Bridget threw her hands up. "Why would I know this or even suspect it? My parents are human. I figured I'd be as well. Odd, I know, but there it is."

Cynthia nodded, unaffected by her sarcasm. "My nose tells me you're something more."

"And you always believe your nose?"

"Always. Werewolves are especially good at determining scents." Cynthia winked. "Each species has basic scents that identify us. You don't smell like anything I have ever encountered before. And that list includes the Fae, trolls, vampires, werewolves, dryads, Ice Demons, the *Morukai*, goblins, and the Water folk."

Bridget groaned. "Faeries and goblins, too? I feel like I've landed in the Lord of the Rings."

"Careful what you wish for." Cynthia winked again. "You're none of those, but you're not completely human. You have some human scents, but not the basic ones, which make me wonder what your ancestry is." She tapped her bottom lip with one finger. "Where were you born?"

This had to be the weirdest conversation she'd ever had with a stranger. "What does that have to do with anything?"

Cynthia shrugged. "It might give us a clue as to what you are beyond your evident human ancestry."

Bridget frowned. "I—This just sounds so weird. Are you suggesting I take it on faith that you're right and I'm not completely human? Because neither of us have any proof of that."

"You mean, other than your body healing so fast it rivals the other Elder Races?"

Bridget snapped her mouth closed. When Cynthia said it like that, she really didn't have a rebuttal. "You know I didn't see that happen."

"No, but you did see the scar and feel the pain." Cynthia waved at her side. "Take a look now. Is it anything more than a thin white line appearing to be several months old?"

Bridget blinked before she pushed the covers of the bed off her body. The baggy sweatpants easily slid down her hip as she lifted the sweatshirt. An ugly greenish-yellow bruise suffused her side around a tiny, thin white line.

"Oh my God, it's gone."

"You see? We're really not making any of this up. Is it still tender?"

"A little. But it feels like it's days old rather than hours."

Cynthia nodded. "So shall we continue on the premise that you're more than human?"

"I—I guess." Bridget nodded slowly. "Are those for me?" She gestured to the end of the bed at the pile of clothes.

"Oh, yes." Cynthia's smile broadened. "I figured you'd like something other than borrowed sweats to wander around in. Especially if you're feeling strong enough to come downstairs."

"You're really going to let me wander around the house?" Bridget reached for the shirt, but hesitated. "Do you mind if I use the bathroom? I'd like a shower before I dress, and I'm feeling kind of icky."

Cynthia nodded. "Yes, you can wander around the house, and no, I don't mind if you use the bathroom. Tell you what. Why don't you shower and come on down into the kitchen? We can finish our conversation there and get something to eat. Werewolves never think straight on an empty stomach."

She grinned and Bridget swallowed hard. "Yeah, I can see how that would be distracting. For me, too. I'd rather you were fed than have you look at me like a snack."

Cynthia threw her head back and laughed. "That's a very good idea. You'd definitely smell better."

"Hey!" Bridget scowled, but couldn't hold it long as Cynthia grinned. "All right, I'll be down in about twenty minutes."

"That long?"

"I plan on taking a decently long shower to see if I can get my head back in the game."

Cynthia chuckled. "That sounds fair. See you in twenty." She rose and sailed straight out the door, closing it quietly behind her.

Bridget waited for the snick of the lock, but it never came. *Maybe she's serious about me walking around.* Or they all waited to see if she'd bolt. But she'd meant it when she said she wanted a shower.

She pushed herself off the bed, half-expecting the pain of cramped muscles to slam into her again. But while she felt a few aches from inactivity, nothing compared to the day before when she got locked in. The memory made her pause. If she was free to wander around, why the hell did Ms. White Bitch lock her in?

Shaking her head, Bridget entered the attached bath and stopped like she'd hit a wall. Polished creamy marble with silver veins greeted her gaze and gleaming chrome fixtures glinted in the recessed overhead lights. The bathtub sat separate from the glass-walled shower and could fit three adults easily.

"Holy shit."

The whole room was bigger than the bedroom and living room combined in her walk-up apartment in Boston. She stepped across the floor and paused as heat seeped into the soles of her feet. *Heated tiles? Damn.* She could get used to that.

She reached in the shower to turn the water on and disrobed, leaving the sweats and sweatshirt on the warm floor. Stepping under the spray, she let the water pound away some of her concerns. She'd pick them back up after she washed, but until then she'd enjoy the heat. Bridget closed her eyes and reveled in the feeling of getting clean.

The twenty minutes she'd promised flew by, but her curiosity to learn what Cynthia and Fredrick thought about her origins spurred her to get dressed. Cynthia had brought a V-necked purple Cashmere sweater and her clean jeans along with underwear and socks. The bra hadn't made it, but Bridget figured she didn't need it if she was staying in the house. She took a few extra minutes to brush out her hair and throw it into a ponytail, the supplies for which she found in the drawers of the bathroom.

This guy is prepared.

She followed her nose and the sound of voices to the kitchen on the first floor. Despite being large, both the house and its rooms felt welcoming and lived-in, more like a home rather than a wealthy person's museum of stuff. The kitchen followed the trend. Orange, gold, and black granite countertops flowed between brushed steel appliances and golden oak cupboards. Stylish track lighting hung from the ceiling over a large granite island with high stools surrounding it.

Three of the stools were occupied by Cynthia and two handsome young men. They straightened up and smiled at her, their expressions filling with curiosity.

"Oh, good, you're here. I made some hot water for tea if you'd like it." Cynthia patted the stool beside her. "The weather's been so dreary the last few days, I felt like sunshine in cup. Have a seat."

"Thanks." She nodded to the young men, but neither of them spoke though they stared as if trying to discern her secrets from her looks alone. *Good luck with that, guys.*

"Are you feeling better?" Cynthia handed her a steaming mug of tea.

"Yes. The shower helped. Who are your friends?"

Cynthia smiled and gestured toward the men. "This is Matt Denning and his younger brother Paul. Matt's my second in command on security detail and Paul's learning the ropes."

"Very nice to meet you." Bridget sipped the tea. "Thank you for letting me out of that room upstairs. I was getting bored."

"And contemplating ways of escaping on your own, no doubt." Paul smirked until Matt elbowed him. "What? Isn't that what you'd be doing?"

Bridget laughed. "Pretty much. It might be a gilded cage, but it's still a cage."

"Well, before we let you get back to your escape planning, why don't you tell us a little more about yourself." Cynthia settled herself on another stool and wrapped her hands around her mug. "Where did you grow up?"

"Detroit. My dad got a job at the General Motors factory building the gear boxes for car engines."

"Did you spend all your time in the city?" Why did her question sound as if she found it repugnant?

Bridget frowned. "No, every summer, we rented a cabin in a little town on the Upper Peninsula near Lake Superior."

Those summers were the best time in Bridget's family history. Her father hadn't been so drunk and stressed all the time, and she'd met her best friend, Kate Blackamber. Kate lived with her great aunt after her mom died. They'd been peas in a pod and spent as much time together as possible. Their friendship had bloomed and solidified even after Bridget stopped visiting Three Lakes.

"What's your dam's name?"

"My what?"

"Sorry, your mother's name." Cynthia waved the word away.

"Abigail Colleen Shanahan, why?"

"What was her last name before she got married?"

Bridget frowned, trying to remember. "I think her last name was Cymru."

Cynthia's head came up and her nostrils flared. Matt and Paul shared a look, but said nothing.

"Cymru, as in "Wales" in Gaelic?" She pronounced it "khoom-ree".

"I guess. I don't know Gaelic." *What is she getting at?*

"What was her mother's name?"

Bridget shrugged. "I don't know. Gramma never came to see us, and we never visited her. Mom didn't talk much about her. Why?"

Cynthia smiled smugly like a kid who'd grabbed the brass ring on a carousel.

"There's a legend I've heard that talks about the Goddess of the Gaels taking human form. My grandmother used to tell us that if we were really lucky, we'd get to meet the Goddess in her Avatar form." She shot a look at Matt and Paul. "The Avatar is meant to help the human race restore the balance of nature, and return to their own true selves."

Bridget raised an eyebrow. In her experience, humans didn't give a damn about nature unless it stopped them from getting where they wanted to go or doing what they wanted to do. *Money and the illusion of power, that's what they teach the kids to value.*

"Each country has a bloodline stemming from the Goddess, and those from the Welsh line came from the

Cymru Clan, Cymru meaning Wales, or the Goddess Herself." Cynthia waved a hand at Bridget. "I'd guess you're descended from one of the Cymru Clan, which would explain why you don't smell human, but more like a pine forest. You aren't completely human if your grandmother was, or rather is, the Goddess."

"Whoa, whoa, whoa. Hold on here." Bridget shook her head as she put both hands out to forestall any other weird pronouncements. "Trust me, I'm human enough. My parents were ordinary, dysfunctional people. My dad was a drunk, and my mother is a normal, guilt-driven Catholic woman who prefers her men manipulative and abusive."

"I take it your father is dead?"

Bridget nodded with a grimace. "Died of liver cirrhosis when I was twelve. But that begs the question, why would the child of the Goddess, if that's who my mother is, put up with my asshole father until his death? If she was so special, wouldn't she have raised my brothers and me with knowledge of our birthright?"

"You would think she'd have passed that on to you. She never mentioned it?"

"No." And Bridget had no intention of asking her. Her sanity was already treading on thin ice.

Cynthia nodded thoughtfully. "You said she was a normal, guilt-ridden Catholic. Perhaps she turned her back on her heritage out of rebellion. Children often do that sort of thing." She winked and Bridget wondered if the woman knew more about her past than she said.

"The Catholic religion did a number on the druids and the 'nature-lovers', as they were called." Matt rubbed his chin. "It was a scary time and most of them went into hiding for centuries. Maybe your mom was trying to hide her ancestry and abilities."

"The only abilities my mother had were making her children feel awful and getting in the way of my father's fists." Bridget shook her head bitterly. "There was no magic, no spiritual pursuits other than Catholicism, and certainly no escape except alcohol. It's a wonder my brothers and I even survived to adulthood."

"Are you a Catholic?"

Bridget snorted. "I gave up Catholicism for Lent one year, and by the time Lent was over, it didn't seem all that worthwhile to pick back up again. I never was into the whole 'guilt-by-birth' thing. Sin doesn't get handed down to us like an inheritance."

She stopped before she got going too much. The old argument she'd had with her brothers, who practiced Catholicism, still irked her. She didn't need to tell strangers, and delusional ones, she'd never felt comfortable worshiping the graphic displays of Jesus's suffering to get a free pass to a paradise. All bets were off if sex happened before marriage, but she didn't believe anyone had the right to tell her sex was wrong, and she'd lost her free pass years ago.

"My brothers and I have agreed to disagree about Catholicism." She sighed and rubbed the back of her neck to ease her tension. "I won't even talk to my mother about it. She goes into this whole 'Hellfire and Brimstone' rant that would make you think she's Southern Baptist."

Cynthia gave her a compassionate look. "That sounds rough."

"It is. And now she's on the whole 'if you were a better woman, you'd find a good man to take care of you' kick." She swallowed against the rising anger. "As if a man can save me from the ugliness of this world." She raised her chin to the men standing with Cynthia. Neither looked away, but they didn't smirk either.

"Was there ever a time when you felt good as a child? You know, comfortable and happy some place?"

"Yeah, those summers in Michigan were the best. Free to roam through the big trees, or play in the lakes or even just sit in the cleared meadows and fields, telling stories and weaving flower crowns."

Cynthia smiled and sniffed again. "Wow, you smell really good, like the forest after a hard rainstorm or a meadow of cherry trees in the spring when the blooms come out."

"Stop." Bridget shivered. "Why do you keep sniffing at me like that?"

"Two reasons, actually." Cynthia grinned. "The first is werewolves are very similar to their canine counterparts, and smelling everything tells us a lot about what's really going on. And second, I know it annoys the hell out of you, which makes you smell more like a forest fire, all hot, smoky, and singed."

"You're so weird." Bridget shook her head, but Cynthia's grin was infectious. "I'm not going to break you of this delusion, am I?"

"'Fraid not, m'dear," Cynthia told her cheerfully while the men shook their heads. "Nor Fredrick, either. We're pretty set in our ways, which includes turning fuzzy, especially when the moon is full."

Bridget swallowed hard. She'd forgotten about the shape-shifting aspect and wasn't sure she'd like to see that. It couldn't be an easy change, what with the bone structures of humans being so vastly different from wolves.

"Does this mean you can shift anytime, not just when the moon's full?"

"Yep." Paul nodded. "We have to shift during the full moon, but we can shift at any time."

Good heavens.

She cleared her throat. "Are you really going to let me wander around the house on my own?"

Cynthia nodded. "You're welcome to explore the house whenever you feel like it."

"What about the woman who locked me in? I'd like to remind all of you I didn't ask to be here or to be kept. I'd prefer to go home. Maybe you can convince Fredrick he should let me go back to my quiet existence in Boston as soon as it's convenient."

"I'll speak to Miss Vértolvaj and remind her of Fredrick's instructions." Her smile faded. "She does have a rather low opinion of humans."

"That's an understatement," Matt quipped and Cynthia sent him a quelling look.

"Thanks again for the clothes. I feel more like me." Bridget squeezed her tea mug. "Did my coat survive?"

"I'm sorry. It was ruined by the blood."

A vague memory of a bloody shawl flashed across her mind's eye as disappointment out of proportion to the loss overwhelmed Bridget. She'd loved that coat, and the destruction of it just added to the ridiculousness of her week. Tears sprang to her eyes, and her breath caught in her throat.

Over a stupid coat? Get a hold of yourself.

Her favorite coat, her favorite coffee shop, and a lousy, cheap book. Rather than explain anything, she closed her eyes and sipped her tea.

Cynthia's hand settled on her arm and warmed her right through the sweater. "I'm sorry this is so difficult for you. I don't really know why Fredrick wants you to stay, but I know it's very important to him, otherwise he would've let you go when you ran."

"Yeah, I know. I'll get over it. Do you think he'll eventually let me go?"

Cynthia shared another inscrutable look with the others. "I think so."

"Why wouldn't he let me go when I asked? What's so important to keep me here?"

Cynthia sighed. "He said something about a vision of you in danger, and he's determined to protect you."

"A vision." Bridget raised an eyebrow. "Like he's a psychic."

"Yes."

When the dark haired woman said nothing more, Bridget groaned. "Oh, come on! It's hard enough to believe in the whole werewolf-vampire thing, but a psychic vampire? Give me a break." She crossed her arms over her chest in defiance.

"What's so hard to believe about the existence of a psychic vampire?"

Bridget opened her mouth to answer, but she couldn't find one. If she could believe in werewolves and the Avatar of the Goddess, why was a psychic vampire any more fantastic?

"Son of a bitch."

"I'm one." Matt raised his hand with a smile.

"Me, too." Paul added his own good-natured grin.

"I'm a bitch." Cynthia winked.

Bridget let out a painful laugh. It was either that or cry. None of this made any sense. "Yeah, right. This whole experience is just too weird."

"I imagine it must be to you. But one thing I'd like to convince you of, regardless of whether or not we can break you of your delusions that vampires and werewolves are a myth." Cynthia squeezed her arm in emphasis. "Fredrick is trying to protect you."

"Because he thinks I'm this Avatar of the Goddess person?"

"Maybe so. He went about this whole thing the wrong way, but he expected you to be as human as you did." Cynthia grimaced. "When you turned out to be more than human, it changed the way he looked at this. But he still thinks you're in danger and wants to help you." She looked at her compatriots. "We all do."

"Why?"

"Because Fredrick is our friend. He's done so much for us." Cynthia sighed. "He has his reasons for keeping you here. Maybe, if you let him, he can explain. He's honorable and a gentleman, but even his tolerance will run out if you push him too much."

"Push him too much? Seriously, I'm not trying to push. I just want to go home." Bridget flattened her hands on the counter. "Don't I get a choice in what happens to me?"

"At the moment, you don't," Cynthia said without rancor. "Our strength and speed can keep you here indefinitely, like it or not. Just trust that we're not trying to hurt you."

Bridget shoved her tea away from her. "Why should I? I don't know you. I don't know any of you. You act all courteous, but you hold me prisoner. You say Fredrick has reasons and you'll uphold them, but there's no proof I'm what you say I am. There's nothing other than your word." She slid off the stool, impotent frustration making her hands fist.

"Where are you going?" Matt stood as well.

"Back to my gilded cage." She paused and looked at Cynthia. "You know, you never told me what a luna was."

Cynthia gave her a compassionate smile. "The Luna is the Alpha female of a werewolf pack."

Bridget barked an exasperated laugh. "Of course it is."

She left them in the kitchen, her thoughts as turbulent as their voices were silent.

CHAPTER EIGHT

Bridget breathed out onto the window in front of her, leaving a perfect circle of condensation. The rain had stopped, but the clouds obscured the stars and moon. She drew a few bars on the window with her finger, glad they weren't real. *God help us if the moon was full.* She grimaced at the thought that she may be related to the divine. *Or Goddess help. I think.* Then she'd really learn if the others told her the truth.

So Cynthia is the Alpha female of the werewolf pack. Somehow, that didn't surprise Bridget at all. Her mind wanted to revert back to life before the coffee shop, and scream, *No, no, no. There's no such thing as werewolves.*

But it was much too late for that. The only thing left to do was figure out how to get out, get away. She believed Cynthia about the food. They hadn't deliberately tried to hurt her. Hold her, yes, but not hurt her.

Fredrick did dislocate my shoulder when he wouldn't let me go.

Bridget sighed, obliterating her condensation drawing. It really didn't matter if she believed in vampires or werewolves. They did, and acted accordingly. Any attempt to escape would be stopped quickly and efficiently. What she had to decide was whether her freedom was worth any price, and that included her life.

Cynthia said Fredrick thought danger still threatened her, but hadn't said from what or from whom. What if the danger Fredrick "sensed" was that of her own hand? Did she value her freedom that much? Could she really kill herself to escape?

The sobering thought settled in as she sat on her bed to eat the food left for her. Could she slit her wrists? Or even stab herself in the heart? She snorted. Fredrick had taken her pocketknife and wisely hadn't provided silverware, so slitting or stabbing weren't options. Hell, since she was really just dreaming, why not imagine a gun or a syringe full of poison while thinking about it?

Bridget laughed humorlessly.

She finished the food and sat up, stretching gingerly. The aches and stiffness remained, but she could move much better. Sliding out of the bed, she shuffled over to the window and sat on the chair positioned for the best view of the dark sky outside. It looked as black as her mood.

Her mind drifted back to her captivity and she shot another look at the window. Her arm felt much better, but she wasn't sure it would hold her weight. If she got out quietly enough, she might have enough time before they hunted her down and hauled her back, probably less gently than they did before. She sighed and rubbed her forehead. They'd keep her, like it or not, and that was that.

She supposed she could just stop eating and drinking according to the Rule of Threes. Cannot do without air for more than three minutes, cannot do without clothes in harsh weather for more than three hours, cannot do without water for more than three days, cannot do without food for more than three weeks. She'd be free in three days if she chose that route.

Bridget looked back to the empty glass sitting on the table and grimaced.

I'd have to start tomorrow.

Besides, did she really have the willpower to kill herself for freedom? Or could she think of a better way to escape that didn't necessarily involve her death?

Maybe I could charm them into thinking I'm docile. All she had to do was play along with their delusions, swear she wouldn't run, and lull them into complacency. She'd have to be careful to keep her acquiescence believable, but in the end she'd catch them napping and slip out unnoticed. They could keep their mythical creature delusions, and she could move away. Out of the state. Out of the country. Hell, even out of her old life and into a new one.

But do you really want to run from him? The traitorous thought came out of left field.

Of course, I do. Nice clothes, food, and a sexy man aren't freedom. They didn't have to be a prison, either. All she had to do was accept his assertions about his species and her imminent danger.

Bridget let those ideas flutter about her head for a while as the clouds scudded across the sky, slowly revealing the moon outside. She watched the shadows grow more distinct on the grounds except where the lights along the paths glowed in little pools of gold. She wondered what it'd be like to wander his grounds without someone chasing her.

What would it be like to see the gardens bloom in spring? Had he planted bulbs for daffodils, crocuses, and tulips? Maybe bluebells and grape hyacinth? Glory, she wanted to be outside, even if she didn't have her coat. She rose and pressed a hand to the cooling glass, letting a condensation halo grow around her palm as she heard the door click open behind her.

Awareness crept up Bridget's back, lifting the small hairs on her nape, but she didn't turn to see who'd stepped in. The scents of spiced apples and vanilla reached her increasingly sensitive nose and reminded her of the coat wrapped around her in her dream. She sighed and continued to stare out the window into the sullen gray evening.

"A penny for your thoughts." Fredrick's voice drifted across the space.

"I was thinking of ways to get outside." She wiped away the handprint.

"So Cynthia mentioned. Why do you want to leave so badly?"

"Why do you want me to stay so badly?"

"You wouldn't believe me if I told you."

"Try me." She shrugged one shoulder.

"I'm trying to protect you from danger, something that could hurt you."

Bridget nodded. "Did it ever occur to you that you and your friends can, and have, hurt me?" She sighed. "What was that line from the panda movie? You may meet your destiny on the road you take to avoid it."

He chuckled. "Wise words indeed."

"Yeah, but they don't change anything, do they?"

"No. You're still safer here—"

"Yes, in my gilded cage, surrounded by werewolves and vampires." She snorted. "There's an irony."

"I cannot help what I am, but I also cannot prove it to you without hurting you, and I don't want to do that."

"Really? Help me out here." She turned her head and glared at him as she dropped her hand from the window. "Aren't vampires creatures of the night? Evil, soulless folk, damned by God? What the hell do you care if it hurts me or not?"

Fredrick wore a black t-shirt with the long sleeves hitched up to his elbows and a pair of faded blue jeans that looked well-loved. Gray cowboy boots with sloped heels and rounded toes covered his feet. Her hands wanted to see if the muscles under the jeans were as hard as they looked, but she clenched them into fists in her lap.

"Despite the stories out there, vampires aren't actually damned by God. Although some of us might think so, given our need to consume blood and our longevity compared to the rest of the population at large." He crossed his arms over his chest, and the shirtsleeves tightened around his biceps. She'd felt those arms around her, and the memory made her shiver. "As for why I don't care to hurt you, you don't choose whom you love, you just love them."

The image in her head popped as Bridget barked out a laugh of disbelief. "Love? You call this love? Good glory. So back in your day, the time of Neanderthals, you just clubbed your mate and then held her captive for a while until she gave up trying to escape, right? This fits right in. Love someone, hold them captive until they acquiesce to your dominance. Excuse me while I cry bullshit." She sat down.

"I told you you wouldn't believe me."

"Oh no, I really do," she said in a falsely cheerful voice. "Because I always kidnap and torture my loved ones, too. Nothing says true love like dislocating a limb and locking someone in." She dropped her head and sighed as she closed her eyes. "Just go protect me from whatever, and leave me alone."

Silence descended around them, and she hoped he'd gone, but the scuff of his boot against the carpet and a rustle of clothing told her he'd crouched in front of her. She opened her eyes to look down at him in surprise. His gaze traveled from her knees up her chest to her face, his expression full of resignation. She hated the twinge of guilt pricking her thoughts and raised her chin in defiance of whatever he chose to do next.

"If you don't believe in vampires, it stands to reason you don't believe in psychics, either." His voice was quiet and full of sorrow, but no less firm for its softness.

She shrugged. "I've never met anyone who's psychic."

"Be that as it may, I've had visions of you in your white coat, with your red hair and green eyes, always in some sort of danger. Many people have insisted they're merely dreams, and dreams are something my subconscious has constructed from things I've seen in my waking life. But I swear to you before two nights ago in Boston, I'd never seen your physical form in my waking moments, and you were certainly in danger."

"Yes, but was I in danger from the mugger or from you?"

"I'd never hurt you on purpose, Bridget."

She sighed. "So you said, but your actions suggest otherwise." She hitched her healing shoulder. "So you're not just a vampire, but a psychic as well, huh? Must be my lucky week. Is reading minds one of your 'gifts'?"

He laughed. "No, I've never been able to do that, much to my own chagrin when it came to women."

"Yeah, it's definitely not working on me." She rubbed her forehead with one hand. "So what kind of psychic are you?"

"My psychic abilities are limited to visions of possible futures of people, either myself or someone I know."

"I'm not someone you know. You said you didn't know me before two nights ago."

"What I said was I'd never seen you physically. I didn't say I didn't know you."

Bridget narrowed her eyes. *Pompous jackass.* She hated guys who thought they were so clever, so self-assured by trying to sound wise without having true wisdom. At least Fredrick didn't wear a smug smirk.

"You're an asshole," she said at last, turning back to the window.

"Sorry?"

"An asshole," she repeated with a snarl. "A jerk. A self-involved, delusional, megalomaniac who's so insecure with who he really is that he has to make up stories about amazing abilities and vampirism. You think you're so clever, so smart, that if you tell me you know me, I'll ask how that can be possible. And the music will swell, and you'll tell me you've known me all your incredibly long life, seeing me in different guises as different people, but always with the same energy and grace. And I'll turn to you with tears in my eyes and say I knew there was something about you that I sensed, and we will rush together and kiss and then the credits will roll." She scowled. "Yeah, I've seen the movie, read the book, and heard the story. The problem is, you're really not that clever, and I'm really not that stupid."

Another silence ensued, and even through her disgust, she sensed his anger building. Her skin heated with the radiance of it.

"You are incredibly angry." His anger coiled under his voice like a threatened snake.

"Ya think?"

"You have good reason, given I'm holding you here against your will. But before you grace me with another one of your ignorant outbursts, perhaps you'd let me finish what I came here to tell you."

Bridget gaped at him. "Fuck you."

"The story, as you so inelegantly put it, goes like this. My mother, despite my father's disdain, worshipped the Goddess for all her life. She had a Priestess bless each of us, but when the Priestess got to me, she took me aside for a special message." Fredrick stood up until Bridget had to crane her neck to look at him. "She told me I would be called upon to serve the Goddess in an important way. Then she placed her hand against my chest above my heart and gave me the Goddess's mark."

To Bridget's surprise, Fredrick stepped back and pulled his shirt off in one smooth motion. He wore nothing from the waist up but a small gold Celtic filigreed ring on a thin golden chain. It hung between large pectoral muscles dusted with dark hair. She damn near swallowed her tongue at the full view of the spectacularly muscular body he displayed.

Holy glory, he's gorgeous.

The dusting of black hair came together in a dark line disappearing into his pants below his navel. She yanked her eyes away from his "happy trail" and back up to his chest before her stare became obvious. The scents of vanilla and cinnamon filled her awareness as he stood before her.

"Cynthia told me your mother's maiden name was Cymru, the Welsh name for the Goddess."

"So?" She offered him her best dry look.

"There are hundreds of myths about the Goddess taking human form to see how Her children care for the world, but I've never met an Avatar of the Goddess." Despite his evident anger, his said the title with reverence. "Look here, Bridget."

He pointed to a large circular mark scarring the skin above his flat, coppery nipple. It was about three inches across and shimmered faintly in the light. Without warning, he swung away from her and turned off the lights in the room, plunging it into darkness.

"What are you doing?"

Her eyes took a few moments to adjust, but the mark on his chest glowed silver. The glow gently illuminated the ridges of his muscles, tempting her hands to stroke the hard edges. When he knelt in front of her, she recognized a familiar shape and it appeared to be moving.

She bent forward to get a closer look. The glowing image of a great spreading tree surrounded by a circle beckoned her, and she reached out her hand to touch it. *It looks like the lapel pin he wore in the dream.* When her fingers contacted his chest, a bolt of electricity shot through her, and she gasped. He gave a deep satisfied groan and pressed his chest harder into her hand.

The pressure buckled her injured arm, and she fell into

him with a squeak of surprise. He caught her and held her close as the energy intensified.

Bridget felt as if she'd found a missing piece of herself. She'd come home to a place of comfort and peace, where everything was familiar and welcoming. Against her better judgment, she relaxed into Fredrick's warm embrace and rested her face against the mark on his chest. Power flared, and for a moment the room blazed with brilliant light as pleasure radiated through her body.

"Holy Goddess!" Fredrick moaned, and Bridget jerked back.

She immediately missed their amazing connection.

They froze for a moment in the darkness, both breathing hard. *What the hell was that?* The circled tree still glowed silver on his chest, a small pool of light illuminating the space between them. Bridget reached backward for the chair and caught sight of another shaft of light sliding over the carpet near her feet. Frowning, she pulled her hand back to get a better look, but the source moved with her.

What the hell is this?

She slowly turned her right hand over, squeaking again as a warmer, golden light from her palm nearly blinded her. She slammed her eyes shut, waiting for pain to strike her awareness, but everything felt normal. Bridget cracked her eyes open and looked again.

The same symbol on Fredrick's chest marked her palm, glowing gently with honey-colored light. She flexed her hand, twisting it back and forth, but the glow never died.

Wow, I have my own flashlight now.

She wanted to giggle, but the silver light cut off suddenly as Fredrick turned away, distracting her. She almost threw her hand up, palm out to see where he went, but when the lights flashed back on, she squinted in adjustment.

He pulled his shirt on over his head, disguising the shining silver mark, and his handsome body. *Damn. Is it too much to ask for him to walk around naked from now on?* She mentally slapped herself for good measure. *My focus needs focus.* Her hand glowed, and she lusted after a sparkling vampire. *Shit, when did I get involved with something out of a paranormal romance?*

"Please tell me my hand isn't glowing because I'm radioactive."

Fredrick's laugh warmed her right down to her toes. "You're not radioactive unless you've visited Chernobyl recently."

"It hasn't been on my vacation plans." Good thing her voice sounded steady. "Why is my hand glowing?"

Fredrick leaned against the wall beside the window, his arms crossed over his chest. He studied his feet while he gathered his thoughts.

"I told you the Priestess gave me the Mark of the Goddess when I was a boy along with a special message."

"Yeah, I remember that."

He gave her a flat look, and she sealed her lips. "Apparently, I'd been chosen by the Goddess through Her Priestess to serve Her in a specific way. That's when the visions started, and I learned to heed their messages."

Fredrick rubbed the back of his neck with one hand as he examined his boot tips. "For the last six months, I've received visions of you in your life, doing mundane things like drinking coffee at the coffee shop, or watering the plants in your apartment, innocuous things. I didn't understand why I received them, but each time I saw you, I grew a little more attached to you."

"Even when you had no idea who I was."

"Even then."

"What does this have to do with my hand turning into a personal torch?"

"Two weeks ago, the energy in the visions changed." Fredrick's voice grew serious, and dread snaked down Bridget's back. "They became filled with warning. I couldn't see what danger stalked you, but I could feel it." He grimaced as he raised his dark eyes to her. "Unfortunately, I didn't know your name or where you lived or even in what city I should start searching. I didn't learn that until two nights ago when I found you at Snickerdoodles, one of my coffee shops." He shook his head in disgust.

"Wait, you own Snickerdoodles?" *No wonder he walked around like he owned the place.*

"Yes." He nodded sharply. "You've been so close in Boston this whole time, and I've only now just found you. I thought you'd be safe if I brought you to my home, the danger averted, but I can't shake the feeling that it remains."

"I'm still in danger?" She rose to her feet and braced her hands on her hips. "But you said I'd be safe here." She shook her head. "Why am I even believing you?"

Irritation flashed across his face before he smirked slyly. "Perhaps because your hand has become 'a personal torch'?"

Bridget gritted her teeth. "Yeah, why is that?"

"The only thing I can guess, Bridget, is you carry the Blood of the Goddess within you, and when you touched the sacred Mark given to me by Her High Priestess, your bloodline recognized the blessings bestowed upon me."

"Wait, the 'bloodline' recognized it? It has an awareness?"

"The Goddess is in all things, particularly you, my dear. She would recognize Her blessings no matter how small." He pointed to Bridget's hand. "The Mark on your hand matches the one on my chest, doesn't it?"

Bridget nodded as she bit her lip.

"The High Priestess told me I would know the Avatars

of the Goddess, those born directly from Her bloodline, when the Mark appeared somewhere on their bodies. I didn't suspect you were the Avatar until I talked to my uncle who's a historian. My suspicions were confirmed when I heard your mother's maiden name from Cynthia."

"Why didn't you say anything?"

Fredrick raised his eyebrows. "What could I say to you? You were already displeased with my conduct and didn't believe when I said I'm a vampire. Were you likely to believe in Avatars of the Goddess?"

Bridget wanted to kick something in chagrin. "No, probably not." She looked down at her hand, rubbing the palm with her opposite fingers. "Will it always glow like this? That might be fun at parties, but a pain in the ass if I'm trying to get some sleep."

He chuckled, and some of her uncertainty drained away.

"I think it will only glow if you connect it to a Mark like mine."

"Thank God."

Fredrick frowned. "Thank the Goddess."

"Right, sorry." The Mark on her hand looked like an old scar, barely visible in the light. She stared at it hard, but she couldn't see any movement like the one on Fredrick's chest. "Why do you think the Mark appeared now? It's not like it was there before just a few minutes ago."

"I can only surmise its appearance is the acknowledgement of the connection between Goddess-born and Goddess-blessed." He grimaced as if he knew she wouldn't like what more he had to say. "It connects us for the rest of our lives, and it's a symbiotic relationship, which means if any harm comes to you, I will be affected and vice-versa. Therefore, it is in our best interests to treat each other well."

"Treating me well." Bridget snorted. "That's what this is? Holding me here against my will?"

"It's for your protection. I still sense danger coming."

"Danger from what or from whom?"

He had the grace to look sheepish. "I don't know. The sense remains, and I cannot take the chance I might not be there to stop it."

She said nothing to that for a short time, her thoughts churning. She rubbed her hand as her mind raged about captivity. But after what he'd told her about their connection, and the damn near orgasmic feeling of being in his arms, she wondered if she really wanted to leave. Especially if he still sensed danger around her.

Do I really believe he's a psychic vampire?

She flexed her hand, remembering how his hand had zipped itself back together after he cut it with her knife.

Yeah. But it meant she'd have to believe she was the Avatar of the Goddess and he was her servant.

"I don't want or need a servant." She wrapped her arms around herself for comfort.

"It's not that kind of service." He closed the distance between them. "I serve you by protecting you as a guard, or perhaps teaching you more about your heritage. It isn't subservience so much as bringing myself and you honor by serving."

Bridget tightened her grip and closed her eyes as the enormity of the truth hit her. If she was the Avatar of the Goddess, and he was her protector, it stood to reason danger really stalked her, and she needed his protection. She wanted to curl into a ball and hide until it all went away, but his approach blocked her path to the bed as his scent filled her nose. She didn't need to open her eyes to know he'd stopped in front of her close enough to touch.

"I don't really understand what is going on and why all this is happening." Fear and confusion overwhelmed her. "None of this makes any sense to me." And she started to cry.

CHAPTER NINE

Bloody hell, please don't cry.
Fredrick's heart bled with her tears and he gathered her into his arms. She smelled like the sour scent of rotting vegetation, and she shook against his chest. Her fear screamed at him from the tension of her shoulders, but he didn't know if it stemmed from him or her legacy. He was one of the monsters she'd been taught to fear since childhood. Bram Stoker had painted a dismal picture of the men and women unfortunate enough to receive the genetic code allowing them to live after death.

"I've got you. I'm here, Bridget. I'll always be here from now on."

He tried to tell himself it was just to comfort his Avatar, but deep down he knew it was more. He'd watched her for months, slowly falling in love with the red-headed woman who watered her plants with such loving attention and read romance novels while she sipped coffee. He'd dreamed of holding her, and the first taste of reality when she'd stroked his chest had been better than any dream.

Her breath hitched, and more tears soaked the front of his shirt. "You've said that before."

"I have?"

"Yeah, in my dream. At least, I think it was a dream."

Every time he touched her, the electricity of their connection vibrated through his body, reminding him of his duty and his desire to offer her pleasure and comfort.

"You've dreamed about me?" Giddy delight uncurled within him.

She nodded, rubbing her cheek against his chest, and he suddenly wished he'd left his shirt off. She relaxed into his embrace, and his heart danced a hopeful jig. Goddess above, he could take her right now, but he had no wish to drive her away with his lust. He had to sternly remind his body to stay calm.

"What was I doing in this dream?"

"You came to make sure I was all right."

"Did I now?" Pride swelled in his chest, but he resisted the urge to push it out. "Perhaps now you can believe I'd do that in your waking life as well as in your dreams."

It was the wrong thing to say. He felt her withdraw from him as soon as the words left his mouth, and he mentally smacked his forehead.

Her scent changed from rotting vegetation to the smell of the land drying after flood waters recede. She finally pushed herself back from him and rubbed her face with her hands. Fredrick missed her soft body against his immediately.

"Bridget."

She held up one hand to forestall him.

"I need time to think about this. Is there any way I can go outside and walk in the fresh air? I think better when I'm walking."

He glanced at the window. The clouds had cleared, and the half moon blazed white against an inky black curtain of stars. It provided enough light to see the contours of the land around the house and the shimmer of the river through the bare trees. The idea of her outside alone made his gut clench, and he had to force his hands to relax from involuntary fists.

Cynthia and her wolves will have no trouble seeing her. Bridget would be fine if she stayed on the estate.

"Of course." He took a deep breath to calm his roar of possession. He couldn't wrap her up in cotton batting. "Just confine your wanderings to the grounds, so Cynthia or I can get to you if you should need us."

She grimaced. "I won't run again."

Chagrin settled into his chest. "It's for your protection."

"I know. Because there's danger around me."

"I realize it doesn't make sense to you, but I've learned to listen to my instincts. They're screaming for me to protect you." He shrugged helplessly, wishing he could convey the urgency he felt. "We're bound, Bridget, and I'll do my utmost to keep you safe, not only because you're Goddess-born, but also because—"

He stopped himself before he said too much. She'd never believe he'd fallen in love with her in such a short time. *She already laughed in my face when I told her I loved her.*

"Because?"

"Because I'm a gentleman, and I can't stand back when I know I can help." He ached to tell her the truth.

"Thank you for your help." Her face belied her words.

"Bridget."

"I'll be okay. I just need to think."

She strode past him and found her shoes, tugging them on in the growing silence. He wanted to demand more from her, but his gut said it wasn't the time. He'd enjoyed six months getting used the idea of her being part of his life. She'd only learned creatures other than human occupied the world two days ago.

She stood and brushed her ponytail off her shoulder. "Does someone have a jacket I can borrow? It looks cold out there."

"Yes. I bought you a new one." He slipped past her to the bureau near the door where he'd set the new down jacket. "They only had it in black and red. I thought you'd prefer red."

"That's fine. Thank you."

He helped her shrug into the coat and she zipped it up, her expression closed. He missed the animation usually in her face, but she hid it from him. At last, she met his gaze.

"I'm trying to understand everything. I just need a little time."

"Of course, take all the time you need. Just stay close."

"I will." Then she was gone.

All the light and heat seemed to go with her. Fredrick stifled the urge to charge after her and hold her against his chest, inhaling her scent.

She'd told him she needed to think and walk, and she'd promised she wouldn't run away again. He had to take her at her word. He had to believe she'd call if she needed him, and he'd hear it no matter where she was on the estate.

She'll be safe here. But the feeling of danger persisted and made his back crawl. He gripped the edges of the doorframe to keep from bolting down the stairs, screaming her name.

Get a fucking grip, MacGregor.

He heard the front door close, and the sound unlocked his feet from the floor. He had to find something else to do other than brood on what haunted her thoughts. She'd come to understand what he told her. She had to. The flare of the marks on their bodies confirmed the truth. Now it made sense why she'd been in his visions, but the danger floated like a hazy phantom on the horizon, just out of sight.

Fredrick gritted his teeth as he left the room and strode downstairs to find Cynthia or Matt. He didn't want the werewolves to tackle Bridget to the ground if they saw her outside. It wouldn't win him any points, and she'd never trust him to keep his word.

His guts tightened as doubt assailed his mind. Would she really keep her word? His steps veered for the front door, and he'd gripped the brass door-pull before he could give himself a mental shake.

She's not running. She promised. I have to trust her. Fredrick rested his head against the glossy wooden surface, inhaling the scent of mahogany and wood stain until his fears retreated back to a manageable level.

Do I trust her? Can I?

Bridget had never once done anything contrary to what she said she would. In all his visions, she'd stayed true to her word and commitments. She may have turned his world upside down, but she'd never been dishonest. He believed her and trusted her to do as she promised.

Fuck.

He took a deep breath and rolled his shoulders to loosen the tension. It would be fine. He had to believe that.

Fredrick released the door and headed for the kitchen. The brushed steel appliances, golden granite countertops, and oak cabinets soothed his irritation. Cynthia leaned over the large island in the middle of the room, but ignored the four tall stools pushed up to the bar. Her attention remained on a thick book beside a steaming cup of coffee in her hand.

"Bridget went out to go for a walk." He tried to keep his tone even, but suspected he'd failed when she raised her eyebrows at him. "She promised to stay on the grounds, but I don't want any of the werewolves to tackle her tonight."

"You trust her not to run?" Cynthia tilted her head.

He nodded. "I do. It's a lot to take in. Werewolves, vampires, the Goddess. And…everything else."

"You mean that you're in love with her?"

He looked at Cynthia sharply, but said nothing.

She chuckled and shook her head. "Fredrick, you've known me for years. When have werewolves not known what's going on? I can smell emotions, though yours are more subtle than humans'."

"I guess I should be grateful for small favors." He rubbed his chin thoughtfully. "What does love smell like? And are you certain that's what I'm feeling?"

Cynthia snorted. "It's pretty obvious. You only get this twitchy when you're concerned about someone you care for. And love smells like..." She stopped and sniffed deeply then her eyes opened wide. "Whoa. You smell like Bridget. Did you mate with her?"

"No!" He snapped his mouth closed around the desperation in his voice. "No, I just proved to her the connection between Goddess-blessed and Goddess-born."

"That's one helluva connection if you smell like her." Cynthia grinned. "And that's what love smells like. Your scent blends with that of your mate. Good for you, Fredrick. Does she love you, too?"

Fredrick sighed roughly. "I have no idea. I didn't ask. She has enough to worry about right now."

Cynthia gave a scoffing growl. "No one has too much to think about to know if they love someone. Why didn't you ask her?"

"I didn't want to push." He shrugged and dragged a finger over the granite. "But I don't really need her to love me. It's possible to love someone without that person loving you back."

"You mean like Szilvia."

Fredrick grimaced. "Yes."

"Keep your chin up." She grasped his hand. "Your relationship didn't start out well, but other than holding Bridget hostage under the pretense of protection, you haven't really done anything to hurt her."

He wore chagrin like a coat. "Yeah. About that..."

"You hurt her, too?"

"Not purposely." He hated the defensive note in his voice. "I was holding her arm when she jerked away. It dislocated her shoulder."

Cynthia's eyebrows hit her hairline, but she said nothing as she watched him squirm.

"And it's not a pretense. She's still in danger. I just don't know how." He desperately looked for something else to talk about and his gaze landed on her book. "What are you reading? It looks like Tolstoy's *War and Peace*."

"Close. It's C. S. Lewis's *Chronicles of Narnia* collected in one book."

Fredrick smirked. "A werewolf reading *The Chronicles of Narnia*?"

"Hey, it's a great set of stories, and who says there are no dragons just because you haven't seen one? Bridget had never seen a vampire, but here you are making fun of me."

He kept the knowledge of the existence of dragons to himself for the moment and resisted the urge to scowl. "Where's Szilvia?"

"I don't know. I think she went out for a bite, but I haven't seen her for a while. Why?"

"I wanted to clarify with her some business opportunities that have come up—"

Sharp fear streaked up his back, cutting him off, and his heart damn near stopped. It stalled in his chest and he braced for evasive action, hissing as he bared his canines. Cynthia reacted to his aggressive grimace with a low growl and straightened.

Fredrick searched the shadows of the kitchen for danger, but nothing threatened him. It took him several precious seconds to recognize the panic had an outside source. His connection to Bridget shrieked with warning and terrified fury, and he launched himself for the door even before his hearing picked up the screaming.

Something had attacked Bridget on his own grounds.

CHAPTER TEN

Bridget stood still for a moment outside the door to the big house, inhaling the brisk air. Winter had arrived despite the date on the calendar. She smelled the changes in the ground, of plants and animals settling in for the cold season. She shivered with unease, huddling deeper into the new red coat.

God. She stopped herself and guiltily looked over her shoulder. *Goddess, is this because I touched Fredrick's chest?*

She'd always recognized the change between summer and autumn, with the cold wet scents of fallen sun-baked leaves, but she'd never been able to tell when autumn bowed to winter's rule.

Damn, now I'm waxing poetic.

She shoved her hands into her pockets and followed the lighted paths she'd seen from her window. The only sounds belonged to her feet on the paving stones and the wind. The year had grown too late for crickets. She picked her way over the damp ground toward the river when the paving stones ended, retracing the steps she'd taken when she tried to escape. Moving water always calmed her and helped organize her thoughts.

Fredrick had called her "Goddess-born," and her hand turned into a flashlight. She looked down at it quickly to see if the mark showed in the semi-darkness, but her palm remained quiescent. She huffed a relieved breath, watching it plume before her. At least he'd been right about her hand glowing only when they touched.

Her feet crunched in the brittle leaves left on an open path through the trees toward the river. *Why didn't I find this stupid trail?* Bridget shook her head and enjoyed the ease of motion as she walked. Her whole body felt great, better than it had in years.

See what happens when you touch a vampire?

Vampire. The word had so many meanings she couldn't name them all. Scary summed up her feelings pretty well, but he hadn't attacked her as she would expect. It did rather explain the glowing red eyes she thought she remembered from her mugging. But it didn't explain the events surrounding her hand against the mark on his chest.

Maybe that's where the blessing connects us. She wondered if she touched him now, somewhere innocuous, whether she'd feel the jolt of electricity again.

The word 'magic' whispered through her thoughts, and she scoffed as her feet crunched on the pea gravel at the river's edge. Plopping sounds dragged her gaze to the flowing water while her mind puzzled through the new idea. Magic?

He said I'm the Avatar of the Goddess. She rubbed her palm against her leg. *Goddesses have magic, right?*

It stood to reason if vampires existed then magic must as well, and the connection between two total strangers couldn't be anything but magic as far as she was concerned.

Especially when he'd said he loved her before meeting her.

Bridget groaned. She'd admit when it came to

Fredrick, she felt overwhelming attraction, and he had a few qualities she admired. But love at first sight didn't exist. Did it?

The sound of footsteps on the river rocks broke her reverie, and she jerked her head over her shoulder to see who'd joined her. The lights of the homes across the river glittered on the water in the growing darkness, but the person who joined her was pale all over. Bridget grimaced and hunched her shoulders, hugging her arms tighter around her.

Shit, just who I needed to see.

"What are you doing here?"

"I could ask you the same thing." The woman's dangerously silken voice floated out of the darkness. "Did Fredrick not say you were not to leave the house?"

"He was the one who let me come out for a walk. Ask him yourself if you don't believe me."

"I don't need to ask him," Ms. Vértolvaj whispered in her ear. "I know when you're lying."

Bridget jumped sideways, her feet sinking into the soft rocks at the water's edge. The cold seeping into her shoes crept up her back with icy fingers. How the hell had she gotten that close without making any noise?

Oh, right. She's a vampire, too. It probably meant she moved faster than a speeding bullet and could smell everything, particularly blood.

Bridget scowled and stepped back onto solid ground, her hands tightening into fists against her sides. What did this woman care, anyway? From what she remembered, Ms. White Fang didn't want her in the house or around anywhere.

"I'm not lying. I didn't before and I'm not now. I have permission to be out here."

Suddenly, the white haired woman hissed just like a snake, making Bridget jump again.

"You smell like Fredrick. Did you fuck him?"

Oh no, she did not just ask me that.

"That's none of your business." Bridget growled, her lips pulling back from her teeth.

"Wily slut. Seduced him, did you? Got out after you fucked him into exhaustion?"

Bridget's jaw dropped, but she forced herself to think before she said something stupid. She stuffed her anger down deep and took another step away from the enraged vampire.

"Is that what you would've done?"

"No, I would have bitten my captor and drawn out his blood until he was too weak to follow." The death's head grin wasn't reassuring.

"Yes, I'm sure you would have." Bridget's anger flared ahead of her panic. "For your information, I'm not leaving the estate. If I was, I certainly wouldn't have gone toward the river. You don't have to believe me. You can always go and ask Fredrick. I'm sure he'd love to talk to you."

She retreated even farther away from Ms. Vértolvaj, but kept her eyes on the scary woman. Warnings screamed in the back of Bridget's mind as her nose picked up the scent of a bloody corpse fresh from the grave, all damp earth and exposed organs. She didn't want to know how she knew that, but the smell rolled off the pale woman in waves.

"I bet you would just love that. It would give you time to run." The icy voice came from her other side, and Bridget froze. "But if Mr. MacGregor wants to keep you, then kept you shall remain."

"Why do you care?" Bridget surreptitiously retreated. "I thought you wanted me out of here."

"What Mr. MacGregor wants, he keeps, and I make sure of it."

What the hell is wrong with these people? First they kidnapped her and held her prisoner then stalked her when she promised to stay. Getting her head around being related to the Goddess in conjunction with the existence of vampires and werewolves would drive most people to seek psychiatric help. *I'm not sure there's anyone out there to help with this.*

"Bloody fucking hell, woman! All I'm trying to do is understand what in the Goddess's name is going on."

"Bloody fucking hell, indeed," the vampire's voice whispered.

Bridget slammed into the ground with a weight on her chest, knocking the wind out of her. Fury ignited in her gut as she sensed the pair of fangs closing in on her throat. Fear electrified her muscles, but she forced herself to relax as she stretched out her hands for anything to use as a weapon.

The pale face above her smiled. "Finally accepting the inevitable, I see. You are just a meal, after all. Maybe a good fuck. I'll have to ask Fredrick when I bring you back. I'm sure he'll be grateful."

Goddess, this woman just talks and talks and talks and talks.

Bridget tightened her lips to keep the words between her teeth as her hand closed over a sharp rock. She shifted it into her palm and waited for her lungs to expand before she smashed it with all her strength into the side of the pale oval hovering above her.

The vampire shrieked and toppled off, freeing Bridget. She scrambled to her feet and bolted toward the lights of the house. She didn't know how much time she had to get away, but Fredrick had been incredibly fast. She suspected Ms. Vértolvaj shared his ability.

Humorless laughter bubbled up at the irony. All she'd wanted to do was get out of that damn house for the last few hours. Now, she ran back to it. *No one said humans were consistent.* Except she wasn't human.

Bridget hadn't gone more than ten steps when the foul-smelling juggernaut hit her again, sending her sprawling into the underbrush of the winter forest. She screamed her indignation and fury as the vampire landed on top of her.

"You will pay for that, you little bitch!"

Ms. White Fang flipped Bridget over on her back and spread her arms out, holding them down with effortless strength. Bridget struggled, jerking against the restraint, but only her torso moved. She hunched her shoulders, trying to protect her throat from the raving lunatic hissing laughter. She groaned and twisted, raising her hips to throw the vampire off of her, but she had no leverage.

"Yessss, sstruggle for me, little She-meal," the woman sing-songed, her face looming closer.

An infuriated snarl tore through the night, and something slammed into the vampire, flipping them both up with the momentum of the impact. Ms. Vértolvaj held on despite the growling powerhouse scrabbling at her. Bridget screamed again as she hurled through the air.

The vampire let go to deal with the new threat at the last second, and Bridget fell hard to her side, her lungs struggling for breath with the impact. The scents of angry dog and pine forest mixed with the foul reek of death, and she decided the guard dogs must be out on the estate.

Bridget rolled to her hands and knees, shaking her head as she slowly pushed herself to her feet. She hesitated, trying to determine what had attacked the vampire in the darkness.

What am I doing? Run, idiot!

She took a few steps before she realized she had no idea which way to go. Her fall had disoriented her, and the only point of reference consisted of the hissing and snarling mass of conflict somewhere to her left. Her eyes caught a dark, canine form clamped onto the icy pale, human shape, and her feet propelled her away from the combatants.

Get out of the way, get out of the way, get out of the way.

Bridget spun, searching for the house lights among the

dark trees, but her attention stuck on more canine shapes hurtling through the black trunks toward her. She squeaked and froze with her arms clamped to her chest as the animals flew past her with rabid snarls.

Like a train wreck, she wanted to turn to see where they'd gone. Infuriated shrieks ripped through the woods behind her and her good sense ordered her back the way the huge dogs had come.

She jerked into motion and fled toward anything resembling light. Fear chased her through the trees toward the only point of refuge in this weird nightmare of magic and supernatural beings. She should have paid closer attention to her Comparative Religions and Mythologies class in college. It might have prepared her a little better for nights like this. She snorted and choked on her humorless laughter as she burst back onto lighted paths to the house. Relief poured through her at the sight of its bright windows.

Almost there.

A hissing boulder slammed into her back, driving her headlong into the ground. Dead winter grass scraped her face as her nose filled with the reek of rotting corpse and dirt. Bridget was flipped over, and instead of spouting a monologue, the vampire drove her fangs toward Bridget's neck.

"Get off me!" Bridget struggled to wriggle her body out from under the decay-smelling bitch.

Agony tore through her as the vampire sank fangs into her throat, and she screamed. The dogs appeared around them, flickering in and out of her line of sight. One leapt at the pale feeding creature, and the vampire closed her teeth together in Bridget's neck. The jaws ripped out a chunk of flesh from her throat as the huge dog impacted Ms. Vértolvaj, throwing her off Bridget's body.

Pain overwhelmed Bridget's awareness, and someone screamed again.

Goddess, I hurt.

She pressed her hand against the torn flesh of her neck in hopes the pain would recede, but something hot and sticky flowed over her fingers. Cold seeped into her body from the ground and pushed the pain away.

Ah, there. That feels better.

The dogs swarmed around her and the undead bitch, but she lost track of the world beyond the pain and cold. Why did this feel so familiar to her?

The world exploded into a cacophony of sound. Snarls, growls, and hisses filled the air. She couldn't find the source without moving, but she didn't have the energy. Bridget floated in a cooling space, growing more and more tired as sound retreated.

I just want to sleep.

A sudden roar split the white noise, and she jerked her eyes open as another human shape hurtled past her with a pair of long blades in its hands. The figure disappeared from her line of sight and joined in the fight, adding more sound to the overall dissonance.

Hey, that kinda looked like Fredrick.

It took too much energy to keep her eyes open and hold her neck. She relaxed into the enveloping cold and fatigue. A pesky voice warned her she might be dying, but she couldn't quite work up the worry against it.

The beckoning darkness sucked her down.

****

Fredrick skidded to a halt at the edge of the trees when he caught the scents of death and damp earth poisoning the air. Szilvia's hunting scent was as familiar as his Aston Marten, but when it mixed with the murky swamp smell of Bridget's fear, fury bloomed within his chest.

The wolves shot past him toward the river as he raced back to the house to get his weapons, his mind churning with rage. Szilvia had gone too far this time. He'd experienced her jealousy before. She'd target any female to whom he showed kindness. But attacking Bridget in his home, where she'd been assured safety, incinerated his compassion to ashes.

He charged out the door in time to see Bridget bolt onto the lit paths of the estate. Szilvia streaked from the trees and pounced on Bridget, slamming her to the ground in a blur of motion. The white vampire flipped his Goddess-born over and struck. Bridget screamed, and Fredrick's blood boiled.

When Cynthia's wolf form dragged the vampire off, Bridget made a strangled sound of pain. The scent of hot, fresh blood perfumed the night air and she crumpled to the ground. The scent spurred him into motion, and he skidded to a halt beside his beloved as fear stripped his heart bare. Bridget lay so still and pale with her hand against her neck, and guilt brought truth to the forefront of Fredrick's mind.

She only became endangered when I brought her here. Memory served up Bridget's words to him earlier. *You may meet your destiny on the road you take to avoid it.*

Grief and fear exploded in a roar as he launched himself into the fray.

He waded in with his blades flashing in a shining blur eclipsed only by his fury. The werewolves miraculously avoided the silver death. He aimed all his attention on disabling Szilvia. Anger solidified into a cold lump in his gut, and he drove one blade through her hand, pinning her to the ground.

She shrieked and struck at him with her free hand, but Fredrick whirled and thrust the second sword into her opposite shoulder with all his strength. Szilvia slammed into hard earth and squawked with outrage, her gaze locking onto his.

Hurt confusion filtered into her expression. "What are you doing, Fredrick?"

It took all his effort to form coherent words around his bared teeth. "What are *you* doing, Szilvia? Why did you attack my guest?"

"The She-Meal? She was trying to escape. I stopped her for you. Besides, she's only human. What does she really matter?"

"She is my soul mate, my true love, the woman of my dreams, pick your metaphor."

Fatigue dragged at him with each passing moment as Bridget's life seeped away into the cold earth. But he renewed his focus on the vampire in front of him. He no longer recognized her. She'd become nothing more than a monster to him.

"You have broken the codes of hospitality in my home by attacking my guest."

Szilvia snorted. "She is only a weak mortal, Fredrick. She cannot be important to you. Think of what we have shared over the centuries. She won't even make it a handful of years. She won't love you the way I do. Fredrick, think!"

Anger thickened into hard steel around his heart with each insult Szilvia spat, and icy calm enveloped his body. "You were never the love of my life, Szilvia. Bridget is."

Szilvia's eyes widened once more just before they narrowed with a deep-seated hatred. "She has blinded and deceived you, Fredrick. She is nothing more than a blood bank and I'll show you."

She thrust herself upward, jerking the short sword in her shoulder out of the ground. Her enraged face contorted as she yanked the other sword out of her hand. Snarling with her fury, she shot toward the woman lying on the ground behind him with a burst of her fetid hunting scent.

Fredrick didn't think, he only moved. His dove for the discarded swords in the frozen grass, rolling over the top of them when his hands closed on their hilts. He surged to his feet with them gripped in his fists and twisted his body toward the fleeing vampire. But even with his great speed, he was too slow. A dark, furred shape sprang at Szilvia's ankles at the last moment, distracting her from her prey.

Thank the Goddess for Matt.

Szilvia snarled and danced sideways to avoid the wolf, but Fredrick got in her way.

She turned her fury on him. "We had everything, Fredrick. Don't throw it away for a human!"

She whirled and slashed with her sharpened nails, but he ducked and spun, reversing the sword in his left hand. He thrust it backward into her body, the impact slamming her to a stop. She shrieked and dropped her hands, her hunting scent dissipating into rancid confusion.

Without releasing the blade, he continued to turn and shoved the second blade through her heart above the first. His hand and hilt pressed against one small breast.

She stared at him with shock and sank to her knees. Fredrick followed her down, his glare as heavy as the knives in her chest.

"Why, Fredrick? Why her?"

"She is the Goddess."

He lifted his chin as he grasped the two blades and jerked them out of Szilvia's torso, the rotting flesh scent pulled from her with the steel. Before she could stand, he slashed the blades cross-wise to sever her head from her shoulders. The white blond head fell and bounced awkwardly in the dead grass, and he spun to return to Bridget's side.

Fredrick almost tripped over her as the scent of fresh blood and decaying autumn leaves gagged him. He dropped to his knees and set the short swords on the ground, grateful he'd stopped the crazed white monster before she did more damage. Fatigue swamped him, and he swayed over Bridget as her life blood slipped away. Dizziness assailed him, and his vision swam, but he gritted his teeth and forced himself to focus on his lady.

"Dear Goddess." He moaned as he touched the wet

place on Bridget's throat.

Szilvia had ripped open a chunk of flesh to make her bleed out before anyone could get to her.

"You stupid, jealous bitch," he growled as hopelessness swamped him.

A canine whine made him turn to look into the amber eyes of Cynthia. She flattened her ears and dipped her head, tipping it to one side in question.

"I don't know if I can save her." He almost shook his head, but some part of him refused to give up.

Pushing the encroaching blackness away, he inhaled deeply and grasped Bridget's shoulders.

"Bridget Erin Diana Shanahan, I call upon you to return to this body. I call upon you as your bound servant and true friend, as the Goddess-blessed attendant to your needs. Take what you need from me. I give it freely in the name of the Holy Goddess." Then he pressed her right hand against his chest.

Nothing happened.

Panic crawled up his throat from his belly, and tears started in his eyes.

"Oh, please, my Lady Bridget. Please, come back to me. I beg of you."

Subtle light began to filter out from between her fingers against his chest, growing brighter and brighter until a small sun glowed on the grounds of his home. Power, raw and primeval, rose up through him from the ground and flowed through the connection of her hand on his chest. It swept him along with its heat and electricity, ripping an orgasmic groan from his gut. He couldn't hear anything over the roaring in his ears. He couldn't even smell the blood soaking the earth beneath Bridget's body. All his senses succumbed to the power and energy of the Earth Goddess surging through him.

Time had no meaning, but when the energy ceased, he collapsed on the ground next to the Goddess-born with a tired grunt. His ears rang, and his vision faded in and out as exhaustion swallowed him. He hoped he'd been in time to perform his duty to the one woman who held more than just his soul.

The wolves whined questions at him in their own language, but he didn't have the strength to reassure them as his addled mind picked up a new voice. It called his name, asking him if he was all right. He opened his eyes to Bridget's distraught face, and relief burned like a candle in the darkness.

Thank the Goddess she's safe now. He offered her a watery smile and sank into the blackness that came for him.

CHAPTER ELEVEN

"Fredrick!"

Bridget's shriek mixed with the whines of the dogs, and she grasped his face, willing him to open his eyes again.

"Don't you leave me here to figure this all out on my own!" She shouted in hopes of disturbing his eerie stillness.

One of the dogs whined in her ear and leaned against her shoulder, ears flattened and tail down.

"I don't know what to do," Bridget moaned. "Why is he lying on the ground? What happened?"

The black dog whined again and nosed her arm, pawing at Fredrick.

"I don't understand."

The dog whuffed a sigh and backed away, wearing an expression of resignation. Bridget frowned as energy shimmered around the black form, morphing and shifting until a tall woman with black hair and amber eyes stood in the dog's place.

Where do the clothes go when she's a wolf?

"Is he still alive?" Cynthia asked as she dropped to the ground.

"What? Oh." Bridget forced herself to look down at

Fredrick's pale face. "I don't know."

Cynthia snorted with exasperation. "He's your mate, isn't he? Don't you have a connection where you can sense each other's health?"

Bridget blinked and shook her head, then remembered their mutual light display in the house. Biting her bottom lip, she laid her right hand on his chest, and the golden light from her palm flared up once again. She closed her eyes and fell into him, sliding through the dark corridors of his body. Life energy flickered, and she pushed some of hers back at him, willing him to take it. He responded sluggishly, but some of his "lights" came back on. She opened her eyes.

"He's still alive, but his reserves are completely used up."

"He must have traded his life force for yours to save you." Cynthia nodded sharply. "Come on. Let's get him back to the house so he can recover."

"Will he recover?"

Cynthia barked orders, literally, at the other canines around her, and two of them morphed into the brothers she'd met in the kitchen the night before. The rest bolted back toward the house. Matt and Paul carefully picked up Fredrick's limp body and carried it after them. Cynthia gestured for Bridget to follow, but she shook her head.

"I can't move very fast."

Cynthia nodded again and took her hand, practically dragging her up the lighted path after the men.

"I think he will recover," Cynthia said, and Bridget had to remember what she was talking about. "He needs to feed."

"Feed?"

"He's a vampire, and he's offered you his life force. The only way for him to recover completely is to ingest blood."

Bridget's face must have shown her horror because

Cynthia rested a hand on her shoulder. "Don't worry. One of my wolves will be happy to donate until he recuperates enough to talk to you about it."

I don't think I can let him feed from me.

She said nothing as they returned to the house. Getting up to the second floor took almost all of Bridget's energy, but she had to see Fredrick settled in his bed. Matt nodded at her respectfully then looked to Cynthia for permission before he left the room. The other man waited beside the bed.

"You may not want to watch this." Cynthia gestured for the door.

"Watch what?"

"Watch Fredrick feed from Paul."

Fear made Bridget's stomach pitch, but she swallowed hard and shook her head. "No, it's fine. I have to understand who I'm bound to."

"Are you sure?" Cynthia cocked her head, her expression impassive.

"I'm sure."

"Okay, then."

Cynthia gestured toward Paul, and the young man sat in a chair beside the bed, pressing his wrist to Fredrick's lips. Fredrick's head turned slowly, and his lips pulled back, revealing longer canines than she'd expected. Then he struck lightning fast, and Paul grunted with pain.

"Are you all right, Paul?" Cynthia moved behind him, watching intently.

"Yes, Luna, he's just a little more enthusiastic than usual."

Bridget swallowed back bile. "Does it hurt?"

"Not usually," Paul said. "He must be pretty out of it to forget to smooth out the pain."

"Smooth out the pain?"

"That's enough, Paul," Cynthia barked, and the younger man focused his gaze on the vampire in the bed.

"I'm sure Fredrick will explain it to you himself, Bridget."

"Right."

"Why don't you go down to the kitchen and get something to eat?" Cynthia gestured toward the door again. "You're exhausted and hungry, and no one thinks clearly on an empty stomach. We'll be down soon."

Bridget tried to protest, but the look Cynthia gave her was nothing short of determined. She didn't have the energy to fight the Luna. She nodded and retreated, trying to understand the mixed emotions roaring through her. She wanted to be at Fredrick's side, but the idea of him sucking the blood out of Paul gave her the willies. She didn't know if she could eat after that, but hoped the food would entice her away from her unsettling thoughts.

****

Fredrick floated in a place of stillness. Pain and pleasure, heat and cold, noise and silence all faded away from his awareness. He existed, nothing more.

Memory didn't return until light seared through his closed lids and heat burned its way through his body, banishing the state of nothingness. He opened his eyes and found himself in a sunny bedroom that looked a lot like his. The light made him squint and he raised a hand to rub his eyes. Usually, he stayed away from sunlight as it required him to feed more often to repair the sun's damage. But this time he welcomed the brilliant glow.

I killed Szilvia. Sorrow stabbed him until he remembered why he'd killed her.

"Bridget!" He sat straight up in the bed, struggling to move the heavy blankets off his body.

"Peace, Fredrick. Your beloved is well."

The voice made him pause. It held wisdom and age without infirmity, but it also held amusement and compassion. He rubbed his eyes and focused them on the person standing beside the bed.

As best he could describe the figure, she appeared to be a woman with red hair pulled up into an elegant chignon. She wore a comfortable gray v-necked sweater with a blue plaid shawl wrapped around her shoulders. Black jeans covered her legs and silver wove through the red strands of her hair.

"You look so much better than you did a few hours ago. How are you feeling?"

Fredrick blinked. "I...don't know."

"That's common in these kinds of situations." She nodded and patted his arm. "Relax a bit. You've had a busy few days, what with discovering the Avatar and having to defend her. Twice. I think you've earned some respite."

"Is Bridget really all right?"

"Yes, she's fine. Well, as much as one can be when they're worried about someone." The woman shrugged. "She'll be better when she can talk to you face to face."

"Where is she?" He searched the room, but saw no one else.

"Right now, she's sleeping. She needs as much rest as you." The woman tilted her head. "I think you're well-matched."

"By our level of exhaustion?"

The woman threw her head back and laughed. "Yes, by that and so much more. You'll make an excellent guardian for her."

"But she's all right? I saved her from death?"

"You did, Fredrick." She nodded. "I'm very pleased with your efforts on her behalf. Keep up with that. There are many who'd seek to do her harm."

Fredrick frowned as something Drake said refocused in the front of his mind. "Is this a time of darkness and distress?"

The woman tilted her head. "In some ways. Nothing is ever all one way or another. There are moments of light in the darkness, just as there are moments of darkness in the light."

"But that's why Bridget's here, right? She's the Avatar of the Goddess." He stopped and scrutinized his visitor for a few moments. "Your Avatar. Oh, my Lady!" He scrambled to bow, even seated as he was, but the covers got in the way.

"Fredrick, relax. Yes, my Avatar, but there's no reason to stand on ceremony." The Goddess waved a hand to dismiss his obeisance. "I never had any doubt about your devotion. And you did your level best to protect Bridget. I'd call that a success."

"Thank you, my Lady." His heart thundered. He'd ever expected to be visited by the Goddess. He'd believed in Her and honored Her, but he figured Bridget would be the closest he'd ever get.

"I do want to warn you about the Sword of God group. They are determined to separate humans from all other species, and they hunt my *Morukai* shamans in particular." Sadness wafted off the Goddess, and Fredrick wanted to weep. "They must not know about Bridget, or who she is, or they'll make special efforts to destroy her."

Fredrick swallowed hard as his gut sank. "Do they know about the signs of the Avatar or how to find her?"

The Goddess shook her head. "No, it's not in their records, but fear and anger are powerful motivators. They make all beings do things reason would caution them against. You'll need to be aware of the Sword of God. Talk to your uncle, Drake. He'll have more knowledge of them soon. In the meantime, rest, heal, and take care of Bridget." She patted his arm again. "And don't forget to let her take care of you as well. She's not the Avatar for nothing."

"Why?"

"Why what, Fredrick?"

"Why didn't she know who she was? Why didn't she know about the Elder Races if she's your Avatar?" He closed his mouth and wished he hadn't said anything. Some questions were best left unasked, but these had been bothering him for days.

"You just want all the answers to the universe and everything, don't you?" The Goddess smiled. "Shall I say forty-two?" Her smile widened into a grin with an accompanying wink. "The answer is very few beings get it right off the bat. Sometimes lessons are needed to be learned before teaching can begin. Bridget needed to learn a few things about herself, about the world around her, and about looking beyond known boundaries. Life has so much wisdom in it, and she'll always be learning as well as teaching. So will you."

"Me? What can I offer?"

"Beyond the obvious? You'll need to teach Bridget about the Elder Races." The Goddess nodded. "And I think you'll need to teach the Elder Races not to lose hope. Darkness doesn't last forever, and light can be found in unexpected places." She rested her hand against the mark on his chest and light blazed between her fingers. "You have the light. Don't forget to share it."

The brilliance grew too bright for him to stand and he closed his eyes. The weight of her hand against his chest faded as energy coursed through him and he succumbed to the peace and joy of the Goddess's touch.

"Rest and be strong, guardian. Go with my blessing."

The echoes of her voice carried him into his dreams.

****

Bridget stared out the window at a dreary late afternoon as she waited for Fredrick to wake up. He'd fed well according to Cynthia, and though Paul had been a little pale, he didn't look much worse for wear. Bridget had asked if he was all right when he came into the kitchen, and he'd nodded but immediately tucked into a large meal.

The vision of Fredrick feeding off him replayed in her head and she'd retreated into silence. She'd been so wired on adrenaline, dawn had come before she slipped into an uneasy slumber filled with dreams of Ms. White Fang. She'd woken with her hand on her neck and vague memories of light and fire, the smell of rain and a fresh spring breeze—in winter?—blasting through her.

She rubbed her neck now, but nothing marred her skin. Not even a scar.

Goddesses, vampires, and werewolves, oh my. She had to accept them as real. The Ice Bitch was proof enough, but when the "dogs" morphed into people, well, that confirmed all the things Cynthia and Fredrick had told her. The Goddess-born part she still didn't quite understand, but Fredrick had promised her to teach her if she wanted to know.

She swung her gaze to look at him in the bed. His beauty still made her heart flutter, even with his eyes closed and his body so still.

He said he loved me.

She recalled her wish to have a dark, handsome knight save her from her life. He'd certainly done more than that. He'd opened her eyes to a whole new world of possibilities, both good and bad.

She hadn't seen the body of the Ice Bitch when they left the yard. She hadn't wanted to. Paul told her Fredrick had beheaded Ms. Vértolvaj in a move straight out of the Roman Coliseum, scissoring her head off between his two blades. She definitely didn't need that image in her nightmares.

Grimacing at the thought, Bridget turned back to the window. She just thanked God she made it out alive.

God? According to Fredrick and Cynthia, she was related to a Goddess. The Goddess. Not that it helped her last night. *I couldn't even outrun a vampire.* Maybe she wasn't supposed to outrun them, being the Goddess's

Avatar and all.

Yeah, I think I'll still avoid enraged vampires, Goddess or no.

Her mind still marveled at the truth that the world contained vampires and werewolves. Perhaps the movies and books actually did them a favor. The vampires she'd met weren't exactly like Dracula. Maybe Ms. Vértolvaj had been a little that way. She certainly had thought herself superior to everyone except Fredrick. The werewolves could change from one form to another on a whim, not necessarily with the moon.

Bridget felt a little slow and stupid. Fredrick had tried to tell her he could prove vampires existed, but he'd have to hurt her. Unfortunately, Ms. White Fang had done it for him.

And it had hurt, badly.

So now Bridget believed. She simply had to. But where did it leave her? Where did she go from here? Could she go back to her ordinary life, ignoring what she knew now that she was no longer in danger? Or was she still in danger despite the Ice Bitch's decapitation? She pressed her forehead against the glass and closed her eyes. *This is worse than an SAT question.*

"There's an easier way to get out of this room, you know."

She turned around to meet Fredrick's open eyes and the wan smile on his face. "All you have to do is go through the door."

She snorted at the irony. "So says the man who captured me, held me prisoner, and managed to lock me in all in the space of a few days."

"You are not locked in now."

"I know."

"Then why are you still here?"

She crossed her arms over her chest as she leaned against the window, ignoring how her gut clenched. "Did you want me to leave?"

"No, not at all. Just curious." He raised his eyebrows and swallowed.

Is he nervous?

"I guess I'm still here because I don't know where to go."

"I'm sure Cynthia could give you a map back to Boston."

"No, not *where* to go, but where to go from this place I find myself—Goddess-born in the company of vampires and werewolves." She snorted and rubbed her hands over her face. "How do you go back to a normal existence after learning creatures of myth exist and you're one of them?"

He shrugged. "I've always been one of them, so I don't know how to answer that. I guess it comes down to your definition of normal. And in my experience, 'normal' changes every day."

"Are you suggesting I find a new 'normal'?"

He raised his eyebrows. "Don't you do that every time you learn something new?"

"Yeah, I suppose, but I usually know who I am as a reference point. Now I don't understand what I am, and I couldn't explain it if I even wanted to." She groaned. "I'm at a weird point where I know too much, yet not enough, but it doesn't matter because no one out there would believe me anyway."

Dread formed a heavy ball in her gut. *I'm so alone.* It wasn't really his fault—well, it was, but that hardly mattered now.

"So you have more knowledge than the human population around you. What is so wrong with that?" Fredrick asked softly.

"Humans are social. What if it slips out? First they won't believe me, and then they're liable to throw me in the crazy house. It's hard to live with a secret you can't discuss with anyone. Not because it's bad or illegal, but because you don't fit in." She dropped her chin and closed her eyes. "My old life is done."

He said nothing to that, and defeat swarmed over her. Acting like a victim didn't suit her, but she'd puzzled over everything and still didn't know what to do. She'd hoped he might have a suggestion. His silence was deafening.

Woo-hoo, he saved me from death, but now that I'm safe, he's cutting me adrift.

To be fair, that was all he'd promised. He'd protect her from danger. Now she was free to go with his blessing.

Gentle hands settled on her upper arms, and she jumped, opening her eyes. She met the chocolate brown gaze of her erstwhile captor, and compassion filled his expression as he stood before her. The scents of spiced apples and roses covered her, and she recognized it as his personal scent mixed with some sort of emotion.

Does compassion smell like roses?

"How do you do that?"

"Do what?"

"Smell like spiced apples and roses. You're not wearing some sort of cologne, are you?" She dropped her gaze to look him over and almost swallowed her tongue. He wasn't wearing much of anything.

"No. I didn't know I smelled like that. I suppose it's a step up from blood and earth."

Despite the nasty description, she laughed. "Oh, yes. Ms. Verto-whatever smelled like rotting flesh and wet dirt."

He made a noncommittal sound and ran his hands over the sides of her face. She closed her eyes again and leaned into his caresses. His lips pressed to her brow then trailed soft kisses down her nose, over her cheeks and one last one on her chin. His scent changed from spiced apples and roses to chocolate, cloves and cardamom as his enthusiasm mounted. He slid his hands over her shoulders and down her sides to rest on her hips as he kissed her jaw line and the side of her neck.

Fear shot through Bridget as she felt his lips settle on her throat, and she stiffened. The memory of the White Bitch's attack stormed to the surface of her thoughts, and she hunched her shoulders to her ears, squeaking like a mouse in a cat's clutches.

"No."

"I will never hurt you, Bridget." Fredrick drew back to look at her. "I only want to protect you, please you, pleasure you, and love you. I will never feed off you. Ever."

"But I saw you."

"Saw me?" He raised his eyebrows.

"Saw you feed off Paul last night, and he said it hurt." She shuddered.

"Ah." The sound swelled with resignation. "Yes, I was desperate and needed blood." He tipped her head up so she could look into his dark brown eyes. "But I would never do that to you unless I have your permission beforehand. You're far too special to use so callously."

"Special. Because I'm the Avatar of the Goddess?"

"Because I never realized how much I was missing until I found you. There can be no other for me." He pushed a tendril of her hair behind one hear. "I've lived a long time, and seen much, but nothing compares to the light you carry, my lady Bridget. Nothing at all in this world."

She stared at him for a few moments, trying to see if he made fun of her or handed her a line. She'd heard something similar from her last manipulative boyfriend, and he always said it like it was some sort of joke. Just a trick to get his dick wet.

But Fredrick stood in front of her with the color returning to his cheeks and his eyes blazing as if a fire burned behind them. Bridget studied him, trying to see everything in his expression. She dropped her gaze to the silver tattoo on his chest. It pulsed with his breath, shining in the light of the window.

Without a word, she laid her right hand over it until her own mark matched his. She closed her eyes and "listened" with her whole body. She didn't know if she could determine the truth from touch, but it seemed like the right thing to do. Their connection had strengthened since he first placed her hand on his chest. She could almost taste the intent behind his words.

"I believe you." She met his gaze and smiled tentatively.

Relief splashed through her from him, and she traced a finger around the edges of his mouth. Desire and arousal flared as his lips twitched, and she stood up on her tiptoes to lay a hesitant kiss on them.

Fredrick moaned with pleasure and relaxed into her kiss, sliding his hands around to her back to press her against his body. She laid her hands on the soft hairs on his chest and tilted her head to allow him closer. His scent intensified as their kiss deepened, and she opened her mouth a little to let his tongue in. He relaxed and allowed her to take the lead on how deep she would go.

Bridget kissed him more, sliding her tongue into his mouth and over his teeth, searching for his elongated canines. When she found them she took her time stroking them with the tip of her tongue until they grew larger and sharper. He moaned again, and his hands tightened their hold on her back at her lingual caress. Something hard and warm pressed into her belly, and she backed off a little. Who knew a vampire's canines were so sensitive?

Careful not to draw blood on his sharp teeth, she moved her tongue down to test the lower, shorter canines. His moan deepened to an aroused growl, and she almost giggled with delight.

Like that, do you?

The cloves portion of his musk overwhelmed his other scents as his breathing quickened. Enjoying her power, she slid her hands downward until they traced his ribs on his sides, and he gasped with surprised pleasure, throwing his head back.

Oh yeah, I've got you now.

In a flash of inspiration, she ducked her head and kissed him between his pectoral muscles, inhaling his delicious scents. He sucked his breath in quickly through his nose and dropped his head to look down at her with delighted incredulity.

She ignored him and trailed kisses across his broad chest to his left nipple before encircling it with her tongue. His heart thundered beneath her cheek as she closed her lips and sucked on it. A groan ripped from him, shifting into an amazed hiss as she closed her teeth gently around the small, hardened nub.

"Goddess, Bridget, if you continue, I don't think I can hold back." He grasped her face to tilt it upwards. "I don't want to force you, but I have only so much restraint to keep myself from taking you if you push me much more."

"You said you loved me."

"I *do* love you," Fredrick said, his voice thick. "But even I don't have the strength to override my baser instincts when it comes to a woman I want as much as I want you. Your body calls to me."

"You mean my blood."

"No, you saw me feed from Paul. Your body is beautiful and full and so…so…" Words failed him, and he closed his eyes as he nuzzled her cheek and jaw-line. "I want to glory in it, to show you I am worthy of your gift. I want to show you the pleasure making love with you will give me."

When she frowned, puzzled, he smiled slowly with sensual promise.

"I want you to see my satisfaction in giving your body pleasure. You're a woman who is meant to be savored and adored." He rubbed her cheeks with his thumbs. "Anyone who simply took quick release from you has done you a disservice. You're the embodiment of the Goddess and should be treated as such, but you are also the woman I care for most in this whole world."

"After only a few days?"

"You must remember I've seen you in my visions for months."

Bridget snorted. "Seeing isn't knowing, Fredrick."

"True, but you've been here in person, and I've learned so much more about you. I love your body, your smell, your smile, your eyes, your sharp temper, the fire in your heart, your courage in accepting what I am. What we all are."

He stopped and stood up taller, looking deeply into her eyes. His scent changed again to ginger and cayenne pepper as the fires of want and truth burned through his voice.

"If you wish to leave, you are free to go. I won't stop you. But know that I would rather you stay forever with me, so I can worship you as my lover, my Goddess, my wife."

"Wait, what?"

Fredrick smiled a smile full of the promise of sex, pleasure, and love. Then he closed the distance between them and pressed the already thick bulge in his boxer shorts against her pelvis.

"My wife if you'll have me." He rested his hands on her hips. "Bridget Erin Diana Shanahan, would you marry me and be a vampire's lover?" He dropped his lips to her collar bone and nibbled the edges of her throat.

Bridget sighed, feeling the lust surge from where she'd tamped it down. His hair fell around her face, and she inhaled the flowery shampoo he must have used. His kisses became more insistent, and she almost let go and let him do whatever he wanted to her. It had been years since a man had taken the time to make her feel good, and she was loath to pass up the opportunity.

"Will you, Bridget?" His voice flowed over her like his

hair, thick, warm, velvety and fragrant. She didn't want to say anything, but she knew he needed an answer.

Which means I have to think. Focus.

Did she want to marry him? Live in his beautiful house, make love to his handsome body, and fulfill her mother's wishes? She discarded the last thought. Her mother had no place in this consideration. The first two things didn't seem all that bad.

"I have a few conditions." She gasped as his hands tunneled under her shirt and fondled her breasts.

"Is that a yes?"

He lifted the shirt over her head and tossed it aside.

"Yes, but first—"

Her voice devolved into a moan as he took the exposed nipple into his warm mouth. His tongue slid over the bumps on her aureole, bouncing and jumping from one to the next without missing the lows in between. She struggled to regain composure.

"First, you can't feed off of me unless it's a dire emergency, and even then we will have to talk about it."

"I told you I would never feed off you." He nuzzled her breast with his nose as he slid a hand over her other shoulder. "What else?"

"Dear God." Her attention was wavering from her thoughts to what he was doing with his tongue on her other breast. "Ooohhhh. Second...Second. I don't share very well, so I won't tolerate you sleeping with any other woman. Ever."

"Oh, my Lady Goddess." He ran his tongue along the underside of her breasts then down the midline of her body as he dropped to his knees. "There will never be a woman in this world who will equal you or tempt me from your glorious body. No ordinary woman could compare to the connection I have with you."

Pleasure flooded through her and submerged the last of her resistance. "In that case, you have until the sun comes up tomorrow morning to stop doing that."

A deep, velvet chuckle rumbled up from her belly as his hands slipped beneath her waistband. "Very well, my Lady."

CHAPTER TWELVE

Elation shot through Fredrick's veins as he carefully unbuttoned Bridget's pants and slid them down over her hips. She sighed with pleasure, and he smiled without looking up at her. His wife. She'd agreed to marry him if he didn't feed off her or have sex with another woman. He laughed inwardly as he ran his fingertips over her bare buttocks. No other woman could ever tempt him from her side.

Bridget let out a soft moan, and her legs stiffened as she succumbed to his touches. The connection between them let him feel her pleasure, and he found it more addictive than the hot, copper scent of blood.

And the scent of her arousal isn't bad, either.

He drew her forward to step out of her pants and rose to his feet to gather her close to him once more as she stumbled.

"Easy, love." He kissed her softly, and she melted into his embrace.

He loved her response, but he didn't want to rush this. She'd granted him the gift of her body willingly, and he wanted to savor every moment. He'd waited half a year for her, and he'd take his time. When she turned her head to breathe, he lifted her with his hands on her ribs and carried her to the bed, his bed, where he'd wanted her the moment he'd undressed her to care for her wound.

His body roared its approval as he laid her gently on the soft sheets, and he again marveled at the wondrous expanse of her breasts. Now he would taste them and determine if his earlier estimate of their sweetness was accurate.

"Are you enjoying this, my lady?" he asked as he lowered his face between the swells of creamy flesh. He pushed his hips between her thighs and pressed his weight onto her.

"Oh, God, yes."

"No. Oh Goddess." He slid his tongue along the underside of one breast while his hand caressed the other.

Bridget arched her back and gasped with pleasure. He smiled around the aureole and nipple and cupped the outer bulge with his other hand, trailing his fingers over the silky smooth skin. He dragged his tongue over her nipple and closed his lips around it as he gently nipped her with his canines, careful not to break the skin.

As she squealed in surprise, he rose up and switched to the other breast, leaving one hand to caress the first. He flicked the first nipple as his tongue massaged the second. She whimpered and squirmed beneath him, but he held her fast and kept up the torturous pleasure, languidly sucking and licking her swollen breast.

Finally, he moved from her wondrous mounds and dropped kisses and tongue strokes down her belly and abdomen. His hair fell around him and followed his motions, tickling her skin enough to make her squirm even more. She looked down at him and tangled her fingers in his hair.

"It is." Her voice filled with wonder.

"What is?"

"Your hair. I've wanted to run my hands through it

since I saw you in the coffee shop. I knew it would be just like silk rope."

He grunted in amusement and returned to his pleasurable task. His hands glided down her belly, feeling the gentle curves of the muscles beneath her smooth skin. He stopped his hands at her thighs and gently pushed them apart so he could nuzzle her mound. She smelled like a mixture of sweet, copper blood, eroticism, and Japanese cherry blossoms, and he dove in, savoring her sweet juices.

Sweet sugar, sultry cinnamon, tangy citrus. All his favorite flavors flowed from her, and he reveled in her tastes. He probed gently at her outer lips, flicking and kissing the hard button of her clitoris.

Bridget keened a high wail of pleasure as he sucked on her clit, periodically leaving it to lick her inner folds without entering her hot pussy. His own pleasure ramped up with each sound, and warm tangy cream trickled onto his tongue.

By the Goddess, she tastes wonderful.

His right hand continued down to her left knee, caressed her kneecap then leisurely slid up her inner thigh and across her left hip. Bridget writhed, and he smiled against her sweet flesh, satisfaction filling him.

He'd found nothing better in his long life than pleasuring a sexy woman. It turned him on almost as much as her pleasuring him, and his own body tightened with arousal.

His lips and tongue massaged her outer folds while his right hand continued over her belly and tweaked her left breast. The nipple hardened under his fingers, and her scent changed from fresh cut grass in spring to sharp pine in the sun as her lust surged.

"Oh my glory, Fredrick…"

He chuckled against her hot flesh. "Yes, your glory indeed, my love."

Fredrick gently pulled his mouth lower and inserted his

tongue into her moist heat while he pushed the tip of his nose between her lips. She gasped in surprise as he flicked his tongue around the smooth sides of her outer lips and wriggled his face so his nose slipped between them to nuzzle her clit.

She whimpered and arched her back in supplication. Her hips lifted off the bed a little, urging him on. He smiled to himself and slid his nose slowly up and down over the base of the clitoris, catching her sweet cream on his tongue with each motion.

Bridget gasped and moaned in ecstasy, rocking her hips to the rhythm of his nose and tongue. He settled his entire weight on her to hold her down as he feasted on her pussy. As she moved under him, he rhythmically licked her swollen lips as he stroked her clitoris with his nose.

"That's it, Lady. Take your pleasure, and come for me."

She sucked her breath in one last time and let out high-pitched squeal as the orgasm crashed over her. He kept licking her, drinking the shockwaves of her release as they came in pulses and filled his mouth with her ambrosia. At last, she relaxed down onto the bed and sighed. He gave her one last lick and pulled himself up onto his hands to look at her.

Bridget smiled at him from under heavy lids, her expression as satisfied as a cat with a belly full of cream. His own satisfaction settled around him as he licked her juices off his lips, feeling cat-like himself. She'd tasted so sweet, sweeter even than he'd imagined, and his cock stiffened in an erotic reminder.

She rose languidly from the pillows to draw him upwards with her, still smiling her satisfied smile. Her gaze traveled down his body to his waist where they stopped at the wet spot on his boxer shorts. Her grin widened as she tugged the boxers off his hips and over his very hard cock, and his heartbeat accelerated. She looked like she'd discovered treasure as she licked her lips, making his lust surge. Was there anything more beautiful than a sexy woman enjoying herself?

"Thank you so much." She sighed.

"For what, my lady?"

"For the lip service and this."

She slid one hand down his body to grasp his hard cock and ran her thumb over the tip. Pleasure flared, tightening his balls against his body.

"I'd ask you if you really enjoyed it, but I think I have my answer right here."

Fredrick laughed. "Bridget, my love, I've never enjoyed it that much in my life. Anytime you want me to do it to you, just ask, and I'll drop what I am doing to come to you."

She smiled again, but this time it was full of mischief. "Then perhaps you would indulge me."

He raised his eyebrows in surprise. "Again, right now?"

"Oh no, not for me, but for you."

Bridget slid out from under him with the grace of a cat then pushed him down in the bed onto his back. Her glorious breasts hung from above him like mounds of soft silk he wanted to caress for hours on end, but she wriggled down his body to settle between his legs, pressing the soft globes against his calves.

She rested on her stomach with her legs bent at the knees and her ankles crossed above her. Her left hand supported her head and her right hand slid up his left thigh, tracing the outlines of the muscles.

Damn, even her ankles are sexy.

Fredrick imagined them locked behind his back as he pounded into her, and his cock flexed in response to his thoughts. She smiled smugly as if she'd read his mind and trailed her fingers closer to his genitals. He sucked his breath in and closed his eyes as she skimmed near his testicles, but didn't actually touch them.

Because his eyes were closed he didn't see her move, but they snapped back open when her warm, wet mouth closed around the tip of his cock and her tongue rubbed the edges of the head.

"Dear Goddess of All!"

Was that his voice moaning? He lost track over everything else as she pushed her mouth down onto the shaft, encasing him in wet heat. Then he felt her tongue snake around and stroke the hairs at the base, tickling.

He inhaled to groan and the scent of excited female saturated his senses, building his arousal higher. Each swipe of her tongue sent a pulse of sensation up his spine and hardened his penis until it felt like a pillar of marble.

She increased the pressure of her mouth on the length of his shaft and pulled gently upwards. Then she released it with a subtle *pop* and slid back down to flick her tongue at the hairs again. He fisted the bed sheets so tight his knuckles cracked, and he wondered where the hell she'd learned to do this.

It doesn't matter as long as she doesn't stop.

Fredrick lost himself in the sensations, the pleasure and eroticism of her caresses destroying his sense of time and place. She brought him close to the brink many times, but just as he reached his limit, she backed off and changed her tactics, building him back up once again.

Arousal built like a wall, a few bricks at a time, and his heart thundered in his chest, tightening his muscles in ecstasy. When Bridget knocked a few bricks out of place, his breath shuddered out of him with a groan as he came down.

When she replaced her mouth with her hand on his cock then licked and sucked on his testicles, he just about lost all control. He groaned and bit his bottom lip so hard he almost punctured it with his fangs, the pain mixing with the pleasure built the wall nearly to breaking. Her touches were soft, erotic, sensual, and he wanted more.

"Dear Goddess, you are amazing."

He felt her smile around his flesh and realized she'd keep this up until he came if he let her.

Growling deep in his throat with lust, he sat up, grasped her shoulders and pulled her gently off his cock. He came out with a soft pop and her eyes filled with surprise.

He dragged her up his body until she crouched on all fours over him and kissed her savagely, thrusting his tongue into her hot, sexy mouth. Goddess, he loved that mouth. She moaned into his kiss, running her tongue over his canines and sending new jolts of sensation through him.

"I'm not coming in that hot, little mouth of yours, my sweet. Not tonight."

When her lips dropped into a disappointed little moue, he grasped her hips and pushed them down onto his raging hard-on.

They both groaned in ecstasy as her warm, wet pussy gloved him from tip to base. He just had enough strength to lift her off until he nearly came out, but she squealed in dismay and jerked herself out of his grasp, dropping hard back around him.

"Oh, my dear Goddess, you're perfect."

She tipped her head forward to stare into his eyes with lustful triumph as she rocked, gently and slowly, scraping her clit against his shaft. He reveled in the velvet grip sliding up to the head of his penis then back down to the base, his arousal building another wall.

"Ride me, my Goddess," he snarled at her. Her rocking gained momentum and frequency.

He gazed up at her red tresses flowing around her shoulders and face as she rode, and love blazed as brightly as his lust. Her breasts bounced on her chest, and her large nipples grew hard at each thrust, but her face captured his attention. The surging arousal in her drew him in and held him fast. The wave of lust and pleasure began to rise, and he gripped her hips tightly as he thrust harder and harder into her.

"Oh, yes, Fredrick. Fuck me, fuck me, fuck me!" She threw her head back in auburn abandon.

Her orgasm crashed over her, and her pussy clamped around him like a hot, wet glove, massaging his cock and pushing him over into his own ecstasy. An explosion of light and power filled the bedroom as they climaxed together, and their bond solidified into a near-tangible rope.

The scents of springtime and exotic incense wrapped around them, coating the memory of their shared pleasure. Fredrick growled as he thrust hard one last time, and then he was done, floating in a euphoria he'd never felt with any other woman in his entire life. Bridget collapsed on his chest and lay there, breathing hard and moaning softly.

"Are...Are you hurt?" He raised his hands to her shoulders.

"No, no. I just have never had an orgasm like that before. Geez, and I thought your tongue was good. Holy shit." She shook with exhausted laughter. "I've decided I'm going to let you do that to me again." She slowly rolled her body off to the side of his, dropping her head on his chest.

His own laughter rumbled in his chest. "I'm only going to do that to you again if you promise to marry me. And I need a real yes this time, please. Then I will ravage you in new and exciting ways for the rest of your life."

"Okay," she replied amiably.

He chuckled again and tipped her head toward him. "A real yes, remember?"

"Yes, Fredrick MacGregor, my handsome vampire lover. I will be happy to marry you and let you ravage me as you see fit." Her expression filled with warm contentment.

Unmitigated joy flooded through him. He'd put that expression there. His life mate and the woman he'd spend eternity loving, both physically and emotionally, rested satisfied in his arms.

"I love you, my Lady Bridget."

"I love you, too, Fredrick." She laid her head back down on his chest and snuggled her body against his. "I really, really do."

"I am so glad to hear that."

"Me, too."

"You do know this means I intend to keep you here in my home, do you not?"

"Oh yeah? What will I do to earn my keep? I did have a life and a job, you know."

"No, really?" Heavy sarcasm coated his words. "And what did you do in that life and job?"

"Oh, I was a project manager and financial advisor for the CEO of a big marketing company in Boston." She yawned.

Laughter bubbled up from his belly. "It just so happens that I'm in need of such a person. I'm currently without a financial administrator, and I have an extensive business in coffee shops. I need someone to keep the books and make sure revenue continues."

"Okay, I can do that." Then her breathing deepened as she slipped beneath the surface of sleep. He kissed the top of her head and fell with her.

CHAPTER THIRTEEN

Bridget sat comfortably ensconced in a fluffy armchair at Night Caps, her favorite coffee shop in Gloucester, reading a set of financial records on her laptop. She'd left her blue fleece hat and matching wool scarf on, but her black leather coat with the faux fur collar and matching leather gloves lay on the chair next to her.

"Goddess, woman, could you make this any more complicated?"

She sighed and put the laptop aside, rubbing her eyes. She didn't really want to think about the financials anyway. It had been a difficult morning—well, afternoon for most people—and she needed a break.

She reached out and picked up her mug, inhaling the steam rising off the hot Chai. The scents of cinnamon and cardamom soothed a little of her frustrations over Szilvia's calculations. Since Bridget had taken over Fredrick's financial empire, she'd had to figure out how Szilvia had done things. She didn't want to revamp everything.

Revamp. She snorted. *If only it was that simple.* At least Fredrick knew some of it.

Thoughts of Fredrick sent shivers of pleasure straight to her loins, and she felt a dopey smile curve her lips. Ever since that first night together in his bed, he'd been the perfect combination of suitor, lover, and teacher. He made love with her like she'd become a cherished gift he didn't want to use up but couldn't get enough of.

Hell, I can't get enough of him, either.

She shivered with memories of their last lovemaking session, and her nipples hardened. Damn, the man was sexiness incarnate. Thank the Goddess they'd have the wedding soon. Then their exploits would be legal.

She snorted. *Well, maybe not in all states.*

Bridget opened her eyes and sipped more of her Chai before she ran over her "wedding to-do" list in her mind.

Just email or call everyone. Especially Kate.

Her best friend Kate Blackamber would be thrilled, but Bridget was still hesitant to mention Fredrick's dietary issues. How would Kate react to the idea of fairytale creatures living in the "real world" and Bridget marrying one?

She snorted again. *Probably the same way I did.* At least no one held Kate hostage when she found out.

Bridget had yet to tell her mother, but she refused until she had most of the details of the wedding figured out. This was Bridget's special day, and though her mother meant well, Bridget worried about her reaction to the Goddess connection.

Not to mention I'm marrying a vampire. Goddess, I hope Kate's okay with it.

Bridget set her mug down and picked up two samples of wedding invitation stationary she'd bought. She ran her fingers over the different paper selections as she tried to decide between traditional silver and white or the more artsy-fartsy look of dried flower petals within the paper. The touch of her fingers released the subtle scent of the imbedded petals and reminded her of Fredrick at his most sultry.

A shiver of awareness worked its way up her spine as

the door to the coffee shop opened and closed, allowing a cold gust of wind to slip through with a new patron. The breeze carried the scent of spiced apples and warm chocolate, and her heartbeat picked up with anticipatory joy.

Conversations stopped as the female clientele observed the man who walked up to the counter. He stood about six feet tall and wore a black leather trench coat. Dark hair fell down his back like a silk rope from beneath a fedora, and the leather tightened against his broad shoulders as he gestured for his order.

A collective sigh echoed around the room when he turned and scanned the tables for a seat. The women all stared at him with hopeful, wistful glances, and the counter woman gazed dreamily after him as he picked his way through the tables. His dark gaze found Bridget's, and the corners of his mouth turned up at her grin of lusty welcome.

Giddy excitement filled her heart as he stopped beside her chair and laid a gentle, but insistent kiss upon her lips. His tongue parted her lips and stroked hers quickly, then was gone. She wished he'd give her more but reined in her inner bar wench. When he pulled away, he shot her a satisfied smile.

"You sure know how to make an entrance." Bridget grinned.

"It's a gift." He removed his hat and coat and sat down next to her.

"Have you eaten?" She stacked the stationary in front of her.

He nodded and smiled a wolfish smile. "Now, I'm ready for dessert."

"Oh?" She blinked innocently. "Is there something in particular you're craving?"

The wolfish smile increased. "Yes." The smile mellowed again. "What are you working on?"

"Wedding invites and financials." She sat back with a sigh.

He raised an eyebrow. "That doesn't make you happy? We can always forego the usual rigmarole and marry tomorrow."

She gave him a dark look. "Nice try. You still have to wait until the end of December. No, I just don't want to tell my mother, but if I tell anyone else, she'll find out."

"Yet another reason to just have a simple ceremony in Wales with a Priestess of the Goddess and have a party for everyone else later."

Bridget considered the idea while the counter woman delivered Fredrick's drink, giggling like a teenager when he thanked her with a warm smile. Several women walked past the table to get to their own, their gazes locked on her fiancé with hunger.

That's because he's fuckin' delicious.

She empathized. Fredrick's aura of power and sex appeal made them divert their routes to come close to him.

Bridget focused on the subject at hand. "I can't. Kate would kill me for not inviting her, and my mother would never speak to me again." She paused and smiled wanly. "That might be a good thing. I can't really tell her you're a vampire. She won't even want to hear about the Goddess."

"Bridget, I'll bow to your wishes, but one thing I will not compromise on." Fredrick leaned forward, setting his cup down. "The ceremony must be done by a Priest or Priestess of the Goddess. Otherwise we will insult Her, and given your bloodline and my blessing, we cannot turn a blind eye to that. If your mother has repudiated the Goddess, perhaps it isn't a good idea for her to be present at the ceremony."

"I know, I know."

She grimaced and crossed her arms over her chest, pushing her breasts up on purpose. Fredrick's expression didn't change, but his scent sharpened with his increased interest. She couldn't hide the smug smile.

"All right. Here's my compromise. Let me get in touch with my best friend and find out if she can come here around the Winter Solstice. Then we can have a small ceremony with the Wolfwrights, Kate, and a representative of the Goddess. We can have a reception party for my extended family after the New Year. Is that agreeable?"

He leaned over and wrapped his hand around the back of her head, pulling her lips to his in a possessive kiss. This time, she was ready for him and pushed her tongue into his mouth to caress his canines. His breath caught in his throat, and she heard the crunch of the wooden armrest under his other hand.

"More than agreeable, my Lady Bridget." He growled when he released her.

The scents of spiced apples and cloves filled the air between them as his arousal rose. Wistful sighs echoed around them, but Bridget only grinned wider.

He's mine, ladies. You can look, but don't touch.

"You gotta get a handle on those pheromones, Handsome. Otherwise we'll have a stampede in here when you leave."

He chuckled. "I'll make sure we're invisible."

She raised an eyebrow. "Is this one of the Noctivenatori powers you've been telling me about?"

He sipped his coffee and winked.

She laughed. "Nice. Oh, I meant to tell you. The Goddess visited during my last meditation."

Fredrick raised his eyebrows and paused. "Did She?"

"Yes, She did." She sipped her Chai.

"Are you going to tell me what She said or make me guess?"

Bridget laughed. "It might be more fun if you guess."

"Wench."

She laughed again. "All right, all right. She said big things are coming soon. Big changes for Cynthia's family, for your Uncle Drake, even for my friend Kate."

"Are these changes good?" Fredrick sat back, his gaze intense.

"She didn't use any other adjective than 'big', but I didn't get the impression anyone would suffer permanent damage."

"It's all fun and games until someone gets their teeth pulled out?"

"Eww, yeah, okay, that's just a little creepy." She grinned. "Besides, I like your teeth right where they are. They're damn sexy."

Arousal flared in his gaze and his eyes glinted red. "Are you ready to go home?"

Fredrick's eyes promised more than just walls and doors. He promised love, protection, joy, and some of the best sex she'd ever experienced. Her excitement spiked, and his nostrils flared as he caught her scent.

"Oh, yeah."

She winked and gathered her things for departure, reveling in her power over the sexiest man she'd ever met. So he was a vampire. He'd agreed not to feed off her. As long as he held her sacred, she didn't have a problem with his liquid diet.

"I love you, Fredrick."

"And I you, Lady Bridget. Forever."

That's what she was counting on.

THE END

Author's Note:

You can find out why Uncle Drake knows about dragons in ORDER OF THE DRAGON, and how Cynthia's brothers, Nik and Chayse Wolffe, find their True Mate in SECOND CHANCE SUCCUBUS, Book 1 of the Capitol of Second Chances series.

ORDER OF THE DRAGON
WARBLER PENINSULA, BOOK 1
SNEEK PEEK

Drake MacGregor always adhered to the adage 'let sleeping dragons lie', until he slept with one.

In an effort to make up for his past as Vlad the Impaler, Drake has been living a small, quiet life in Three Lakes. As the town's archivist, his knowledge of history and his place in it weigh on him. Drake has one desire—to rectify the atrocities committed in the name of his knightly order. Too bad he can't keep his hands, or his fangs, off the local doctor, especially when he discovers she's an actual dragon.

Aliandra Cantora del Viento is old enough and wise enough to ignore her attraction to the handsome historian, especially when her heart suggests he might be something more than he appears. Drake stokes her fires and curls her tail, and after a hot night in her clinic, the game is on. But he avoids her and nothing she tries breaks through his reserve, despite his obvious interest. He turns her on then apologizes for it, repeatedly. Not exactly the kind of relationship she'd hoped for yet she can't walk away.

When a mysterious researcher arrives with his son, Drake becomes more edgy and irritable, and Aliandra must decide if she's willing to fight for him. Especially when he might be her True Mate.

SECOND CHANCE SUCCUBUS
CAPITOL OF SECOND CHANCES, BOOK 1
SNEEK PEEK

Everyone deserves a second chance...

As an ancient succubus, Lady Aislynn is cursed to survive off sexual energy for eternity. To live without killing, Aislynn runs the Underground, a pleasure club in Las Vegas where she safely feeds on the ample eroticism of her patrons. A murder inside her club threatens the haven she's built, even as it brings unwanted attention—and possible salvation—in the form of two handsome brothers, both in search of the truth.

Werewolves Chayse and Nik Wolffe haven't seen each other in five years, and the last place they expect to cross paths is a strip club. The detective and PI find their cases intertwining around the enticing Aislynn and her club. Nik may believe in Aislynn's innocence, but Chayse knows all too well the destructive power of a succubus. He's determined to keep himself and Nik free of her spell.

Nik's missed sharing lovers with his brother, but Chayse seems dead-set against reconciling the past or building a future. Luckily fate, and the Goddess, may have plans for the two embattled werewolves and the succubus with love enough for them both.

OTHER BOOKS BY SIOBHAN MUIR

Queen Bitch of the Callowwood Pack (from Siren Publishing)
Not a Dragon's Standard Virgin (from Siren Publishing)

Cloudburst Colorado Series
A Hell Hound's Fire (from Three Lakes Books)
The Beltane Witch (from Three Lakes Books)
Christmas I.C.E. Magic (Happy Holidays from the Crescent
Moon Lodge Anthology)
Cloudburst Ice Magic (from Three Lakes Books)

Rifts Series
Take the Reins (from Three Lakes Books)
A Centaur's Solstice Wish (from Three Lakes Books)

Bad Boys of Beta Squad Series
Bronco's Rough Ride (from Three Lakes Books)
The Navy's Ghost (from Three Lakes Books)
Rimshot's Hard Target (KindleWorlds Crossover)
Bam-Bam's Inked Hart

The Ivory Road
A Walk in the Sand (from Three Lakes Books)
Outback Dreams (from Three Lakes Books)

Current Stand-alones
Order of the Dragon (Warbler Peninsula #1)
Second Chance Succubus (Capitol of Second Chances #1)
Darwin's Evolution (KindleWorlds Crossover)

Coming Soon
Rope a Falling Star
The Valkyrie's Sword (Warbler Peninsula #2)

ABOUT THE AUTHOR

Siobhan Muir lives in Cheyenne, Wyoming, with her husband, two daughters, and a vegetarian cat she swears is a shape-shifter, though he's never shifted when she can see him. When not writing, she can be found looking down a microscope at fossil fox teeth, pursuing her other love, paleontology. An avid reader of science fiction/fantasy, her husband gave her a paranormal romance for Christmas one year, and she was hooked for good.

In previous lives, Siobhan has been an actor at the Colorado Renaissance Festival, a field geologist in the Aleutian Islands, and restored inter-planetary imagery at the USGS. She's hiked to the top of Mount St. Helens and to the bottom of Meteor Crater.

Siobhan writes kick-ass adventure with hot sex for men and women to enjoy. She believes in happily ever after, redemption, and communication, all of which you will find in her paranormal romance stories.

Connect with Siobhan online at:
http://siobhanmuir.com
http://www.facebook.com/siobhan.muir.35
http://www.tsu.co/SiobhanMuir
http://twitter.com/SiobhanMuir
http://siobhanmuir.blogspot.com
http://pinterest.com/siobhanmuir.35

www.ingramcontent.com/pod-product-compliance
Lightning Source LLC
Chambersburg PA
CBHW070550180626
46817CB00005B/1781